THE GOLDEN KISS

If you are a bank clerk who dabbles in Black Magic
you may reasonably expect your own *modus
vivendi* to be upset. If your wife starts sharing your
bed with a thumping crook while you find yourself
at the head of an organisation whose methods and
objects are decidedly infamous, should you be
surprised?

Not according to Anthony Carson, whose eye for
the bizarre is only matched by his ability to
conjure it up out of nothing wherever he travels.
In this devastating sequel to his first Soho saga,
The Adventures of Mr Quick, he once again
stays put and tells a full-length story.
If the wit, fantasy and surprise twists have a
whiff of Apuleius about them, Carson's vivid
bestiary of London's demi-monde jungle (with
some surprisingly Top People thrown in) is
authentically modern in flavour.

THE
GOLDEN
KISS

Anthony Carson

Methuen & Co Ltd, 11 New Fetter Lane, London EC4

First published in 1966 by
Methuen & Co Ltd,
11 New Fetter Lane, London EC4

© 1966 by Anthony Carson

Printed in Great Britain by
Clarke, Doble & Brendon, Plymouth

PREFACE

All the events related in this book are founded
entirely on fact. None of the characters are
fictitious.
The insertions entitled 'CENSORED' are not
intended to underline something 'suggestive',
but to point a finger at the poverty of imagination
and the hypocrisy of our law-givers.

A.C.

PART ONE

One

I had known Richard Gold for quite a time before he told me he practised Black Magic. 'Not that I've ever had any results,' he said, 'but it's like scientific research, suddenly you stumble on something.'

'I don't believe in it,' I said.

'You don't have to believe in it,' said Gold. 'You don't have to believe in microwaves or nuclear fission. You just use them.'

We were drinking beer in a little pub in Edgware near the bank where he worked as some sort of junior clerk. We were waiting for Stella, Richard's wife who was shopping for a vacuum cleaner. 'What are you trying to use?' I asked him.

'Forces,' said Richard. 'There are pockets of forces in the world you can tap like a fluid. You find them mostly in battlefields, cemeteries or emotionally charged processions. Armistice Day is good, so are Labour Day, Royal Visits and murder trials.'

'But how do you tap them?' I asked.

'By traditional means, tried and accepted,' said Gold. 'Amulets, sacrifices, simulacra and perversion of the Prayer Book.'

I looked at him carefully. He didn't look in the slightest like a Black Magician. He was thirty years old, neat, conventionally dressed and methodical in his ways. There was a hint of timidity in his expression, but he had a very pleasant smile and an air of supercharged curiosity. It was this which saved him from being dull. 'I am not a neurotic,' he said. 'I am not a defrocked priest and I don't whip virgins in Epping Forest on Candlemas Eve.' We both looked up and saw Stella approaching. 'Have you bought the vacuum cleaner?'

'Of course not,' said Stella. 'How on earth could I buy a vacuum cleaner in four hours?'

'I'm sorry,' said Richard. There was a short silence, and then Richard bought her a drink.

'I suppose you've been talking to Anthony about Black Magic,' she said.

'As a matter of fact I have,' said Richard.

'I knew it,' said Stella, and there was another silence.

'I told him I wasn't a neurotic,' said Richard.

'It's a pity you're not,' said Stella, 'then it might be more fun.'

'Fun?' I said.

'Yes, fun,' said Stella. She turned to me. 'Do you believe in magic?'

'I don't know,' I said.

'I do,' said Stella. 'When people are devoid of everything they invent a formula. This is one of them.'

'What sort of people?' asked Richard.

'People who can't dance or sing or be poets, or fight or love,' said Stella. 'Give me another drink.'

'You're in a very bad temper,' said Richard.

'It's the vacuum cleaner,' I said.

'It's because Stella thinks I'm a failure,' said Richard.

'I don't mind unpaid gas bills or mice in the kitchen,' said Stella rather loudly, 'as long as the thoughts are right.'

There was another silence. 'Must I write a novel?' asked

Richard, 'and pretend I know what ten people are thinking in a Georgian manor house in the Cotswolds? As for poems, each one has to be drawn out like a tooth that can never be replaced. It's more honest to work in a bank and have a hobby.' He looked at his watch and finished his drink. 'I must get back to the bank,' he said. 'I shan't be long.'

'If it was only another woman,' said Stella. 'If it was only something you could understand, you could share.'

'Other men have football, vintage cars, stamps, electronic gear, or they get drunk,' I said. 'They beat you or tell you funny stories or lose all their money on horses. Worst of all, they explain over and over again what made them what they are.' Stella was quite pretty, even though she didn't dress very well, she was the sort of woman who really should have cared about clothes. An affair? The idea crossed my mind, but I rejected it, some flowers don't come up in London, some music you can't even hear. The only thing to do, then, is to jump on a boat and look for the Spring again. 'It sounds silly,' I said, 'but do you love him?'

'You can't really love somebody who isn't a bit pathetic,' said Stella, 'you know, falling over and breaking resolutions. Or brutal either.'

'You like brutal men?' I said.

'Not starkly so, just a shadow,' said Stella. 'Richard is somehow fundamentally pleased with himself. Pleased with his lot. Terribly neat and controlled—and then there's this Satanic Black Magic rolling over the uncharted hills beyond the bank ledger. Yes, I do love him. I'm glad he's not pathetic or brutal or displeased with himself. I couldn't bear him to disappear.'

I went to the bank later to cash a cheque and had a word with Richard over the counter. He was flicking through an

11

enormous wad of five pound notes, a great rustle of dreams, but his expression was cool and clinical like a doctor's on a routine check. 'I'm doing an Experiment tonight,' he said, writing a number on one of the notes. 'Would you like to come along?'

'Where is it happening?' I asked.

'In the house,' he said. 'Stella's going out to see some friends. It might be quite interesting, and I honestly think something should happen.'

'I'm not keen,' I said, 'not really. I'd thought of seeing that Garbo film.'

'I want to convince you,' said Richard almost in an anxious voice. 'You of all people.'

'Very well,' I said.

I went around to his house at eight o'clock and Richard took me into the living-room. There was a sort of image in the middle of the floor. It was made of straw and resembled some sort of bird. There was a smell in the air which suddenly made me shiver, not exactly from fear, but from recognition, returning, starting again from the beginning. It was like an ocean wind, wood smoke, forest spice, it was the smell of rain on parched bracken. I took a quick hold on myself and laughed. Obviously I'd made it all up. I am a writer and you can't stop the mechanism working. 'What are you laughing at?' said Richard angrily. 'That bird?'

'No,' I said, 'I was laughing at myself. I could hear myself imagining something because you want me to imagine something. It's a form of politeness.'

'I do want you to understand something,' said Richard. 'It's something very important.'

'Tell me,' I said. Richard sat down and lit a cigarette.

'There's no need to go on about Wittgenstein,' he said, 'and all that. We know there are two worlds, the one you measure and the one you experience. And we know that a number of well-meaning people try to mix the two together, which is absolutely impossible. That is why the Christian religion has failed. What I want you to understand is that there is something else.'

'What?' I asked.

'There is a third face,' said Richard, 'and I'll tell you what it is. It's the non-human face.'

'I don't understand a bit,' I said.

'It's simple,' said Richard, 'It's inorganic and organic awareness of existence that has nothing to do with man. A tree, for instance, a beetle or a bird or a rock.'

'It's a waste of time,' I said, after a pause. 'You're escaping.'

'Of course I'm escaping,' said Richard.

'Drugs or women would be more honest,' I said, 'or simply admitting you're a sad man trapped in a doomed world. Or why not make some money, or even steal it?'

'I could see all those moves ahead,' said Richard. 'I know all the moves for seducing a woman and the moves for getting rid of her and the guilt and the expense of energy, and I know all the brilliant words one can write about nothing that die in the public libraries, and I know the sadistic fun of cheating and robbing. But it's not for me. I'm going to get outside it.'

'And there is Stella,' I said, at the risk of sounding like a Woman's magazine.

'Of course there's Stella,' said Richard. 'And that's the whole point. When I first knew her she was my mirror and I found who I was. It was terrible to be away from her for even an hour because I needed to reassure myself. That's sex for you, and whenever I made love to another woman, I had an utter longing to jump out of bed and find my mirror. In fact I always told Stella everything that ever happened, and there I was, safe and sound, I was inside her. But then I changed. I don't mean that I changed towards her, or became cold. I mean that I became a different person. The mirror was somewhere else. I had to find it. Do you see?' I didn't, but I said nothing. 'I could never *leave* Stella in the accepted sense of the word, I couldn't walk out on her and ask her round for tea on Thursdays. I couldn't insult that thing. So I knew I had to disappear to another point in the cosmos.'

'What you mean is,' I said, 'that you have fallen out of love with your wife, like millions of people do, and you not only refuse to face the music, but you don't even have the courage to try again with someone else. So you visit graveyards and try to change yourself into a beetle.'

'Not a beetle,' said Richard, 'an albatross.'

'An albatross,' I cried.

'An albatross,' repeated Richard, moving his hand gently up and down.

'Let's agree,' I said, 'that you might succeed in your experiment. What then? What have you gained?'

'Wings,' said Richard. 'And what about the albatross?' I asked. 'If you change into an albatross, where does the albatross go?'

'I'd rather not think about *that*,' said Richard. 'And now I'm going to start the experiment.'

He lay down on the floor, extended his hands and said a few words in a language I couldn't understand. Then he lit a magnesium flare and the lights went out. There was an enormous shout and I seemed to be hit in the face by a wave. Then the lights went on. I jumped up and saw Richard still lying on the floor. He was unconscious. I stood there, un-

14

decided what to do. He might have been dead or dying, but when I knelt down beside him I could hear faint breathing. Then he opened his eyes and sat up.

'Where am I?' he asked, glaring at me.

'Don't be silly,' I said. 'You know where you are. You're at home.'

'What home?' said Richard. 'You're in 17 Everton Gardens, Swiss Cottage,' I said, laughing.

'Who am I?' shouted Richard Gold clutching my arm.

'Richard Gold,' I said. But I was not laughing. By now I was absolutely certain that the man in front of me was not Richard Gold at all.

Two

AS I am a free-lance writer I mix around quite a bit and even have a few friends in what is known as the 'underworld', particularly in the North London area and Soho. The North London groups are more conventional, family-loving and violent than the Soho gangs and, generally speaking, drink a lot more. They're not on the social fringe, like the Soho fellows who are more inclined to deal with very off-beat matters indeed and commit mayhem in a sophisticated manner. They don't dismiss Picasso as a joke, as they do in North L., or roar with laughter if you mention Oscar Wilde.

15

One evening I called around at the Way Out in Frith Street, mainly because I knew one of the barmen who had worked in a public house in Camden Town when I had been down and out trying to write a History of the Venetian Republic up to 1612. He was a sympathetic chap called Ron who used to slip me free drinks. This particular room had a juke box with a few hundred pop records and you would never find a religious group among them, whether Methodist, M.R.A. or Salvation Army. This was a strict rule imposed by the owner, 'Grey' Jackson, because beat hymns and revivalist lyrics lowered the temperature of his establishments and took people's minds off sex, gambling or drugs.

'How is "Grey"?' I asked Charles, the barman.

'He's in a funny state,' said Charles. I had met 'Grey' Jackson three or four times before. I hadn't liked him, but then there was nothing about him to like, he was squat, bald, and his stony antediluvian eyes could X-ray a man's wallet in three seconds flat. But women adored him and the further he hurled them away the quicker they crawled back. He owned four or five establishments which dealt with the majority of illegal requirements, gradually ascending in the social scale until you reached the Coronet where evening dress was essential and it was considered odd to bring your own wife.

I was talking to Charles and drinking another brandy when 'Grey' Jackson came into the club and stood by the door. I could feel him staring at me. 'Hullo,' I said, uncertainly.

'Good evening,' he said. 'As a matter of fact you are the man I want.'

'What is it?' I asked.

'I've got something to say to you,' he said. 'Come into

the office.' I followed him out of the room into his hideous private sanctum which was crammed with leather armchairs and photographs of boxers and prima donnas. Over his head there was even a huge reproduction of the Queen wearing the Order of the Garter.

'What is it?' I asked.

'Sit down,' said 'Grey'. 'I'd give you a cigar if I knew where he kept them.'

'If you knew where who kept them?' I said.

'Where "Grey" Jackson kept them,' said 'Grey' Jackson.

'But you are "Grey" Jackson,' I said.

'I'm not,' said Jackson gloomily.

'Then who are you?' I asked.

'I'm Richard Gold,' said Jackson.

'Prove it,' I said, staring hard at 'Grey's' hideous monolithic face.

'Of course I can prove it,' said Jackson. 'The albatross, Stella, the bank in Swiss Cottage.'

'I want more proof,' I said, feeling suddenly cold and clammy.

'The experiment in my house. The straw bird.'

I clutched the sides of the armchair and couldn't speak for stammering. 'You are Richard Gold,' I said.

'I am Richard Gold,' said 'Grey' Jackson.

He began telling me about his new life. He had to be very careful, peering cautiously at everything and everybody from behind his new grey ugly face. 'I have a wife,' he said. 'Her name is Phyllis, and I have three or four mistresses. I go to church every Sunday, would you believe it? And apparently I've got to kill a man in Stepney called "Bugs" Norton.'

'Why?' I asked.

'Ask me,' said Gold-Jackson, 'but apparently I have to do

it. The girls say so, and all my so-called lieutenants who run the brothels.'

I couldn't think of anything to say for a long time. Then I blurted out a remark which was hardly in good taste. 'It's rather a far call from being an albatross, isn't it?'

Gold-Jackson groaned and put his head in his hands. 'Perhaps it's just a stage. A test,' he said. 'But there's one good factor about it. "Grey" Jackson has made an enormous amount of money. I've been going through the accounts, and his blackmail allotment amounts to more than five hundred thousand pounds.'

'Splendid,' I said, and couldn't control a certain excitement, 'but I thought you didn't care about money,'

'It's not that I care about money,' cried Gold-Jackson, 'but, as you know, I am a neat person, and money manipulation has been my profession. Since I can't change my new identity, I intend to give a good account of it, and then, perhaps, the Shades who control the issues of life and death will give me the freedom I am asking for.'

'What do I call you?' I asked. 'I mean do I refer to you as Richard Gold or "Grey" Jackson?'

'From now on I'm "Grey" Jackson,' cried 'Grey' Jackson.

'For God's sake never think of me as Gold again. Don't even mention the name to a living soul.'

'All right, Jackson,' I said.

'But I want you to hang around here,' said 'Grey'. 'It's essential that you stick by me, otherwise I'm done for. Slowly sorting things out and finding out who's who. Particularly this business of killing this "Bugs" Norton in Stepney. Have you ever heard of "Bugs" Norton? I haven't.'

'I haven't,' I said, 'and you're not going to kill him.'

'I am,' said Jackson. 'It's in the part.'

'We'll see,' I said.

Jackson eventually found the cigars and we both sat in the horrible sanctum, smoking. The cigars were very good, and Jackson even sank back in his armchair with an air of satisfaction and calmness. I couldn't help thinking how exactly he not only resembled Jackson but exuded his personality. 'I want you to help me with a girl called Lena,' he said suddenly. 'I want you to find out what makes her tick.'

'Who is Lena?' I asked. 'She's one of my staff. You could call her a hostess. But she's cleverer than that. We'll go and meet her now, and then I'll leave you with her. She's in the Cobalt room.'

We left the sanctum and climbed up a flight of dingy stairs and then along a corridor which suddenly became carpeted and where there were discreet wall lamps. We came to a dark blue door and Jackson produced a key—'I already know this bit,' he said proudly, and opened it. We walked into a large room reeling with music and winking with shrouded table lights. The band was playing 'A Nightingale sang in Berkeley Square', and playing it well; it almost made me nostalgic, but not really, I am not really that sort. 'It's all thirties,' said Jackson, 'a sort of refuge. A softener up, if you like. The clientele are mostly well over middle-age, but you get a sprinkling of young people, oddly enough a fair number of gigolos. I suppose they're fascinated by the idea of the past.'

He jerked his head towards a table at the far end of the room. 'There's Lena,' he said. I saw a fair girl and even by the glow-worm light of her table lamp she started to send messages through my nerves. Oddly enough she made me think of a daffodil, but a daffodil who had escaped from

19

dreamy classical lawns and been shocked into a sharp and merry subtlety. We sat down at her table. 'I want to introduce you to Anthony Carson. He's a writer, and a very good friend of mine. You can talk to him absolutely freely.'

'I didn't know you had any friends,' said Lena lightly.

'I want them,' said 'Grey', 'and in any case I consider you as a friend of mine.'

'Oddly enough, I suppose you are,' she said. She laughed suddenly and then stopped and picked at her cold salmon.

'I'll leave you two together,' said Jackson, rising and looking at me with a sudden star-lit frown of hopelessness, as though I was examining him through a radar telescope a million light years away. He moved off towards another blue door at the far end of the room and I sat down and looked at Lena.

'So here we are,' said Lena. It was a perfectly flippant remark, but it made me feel as if I had made a conquest, and at least thirty years rolled off my back.

'At last,' I said.

'If "Grey" says you are a friend of his, it's good enough for me,' said Lena. She must have been about twenty-three years old and I couldn't think what she was doing here. 'So you're a writer,' she continued. 'Are you a phoney?'

'What a question,' I said.

'It's a very good question,' said Lena. 'This place is infested by writers. Old gentlemen with carnations in their buttonholes writing their memoirs. Their aunts' rose gardens and Monte Carlo. Or generals dictating millions of words about the desert.'

'Not guilty,' I said.

'Then there's Ambrose Glass, the columnist. He can cry

20

in three seconds flat if you mention injustice in Bermondsey. I've seen it with my own eyes.'

'I write a certain kind of short stories,' I said.

Lena finished her salmon and sipped from her glass of white wine. 'What are you really doing here?' I asked.

'I'll tell you,' said Lena. 'I came here some time ago to investigate Jackson's financial situation. I am an Inland Revenue official.' She took another sip of wine. 'Or at least I was.' She laughed and looked at me with a mocking yet open look. 'I trust you,' she said, 'and I'll tell you everything. After a month's investigation of Jackson's financial position I discovered that his position, legally, was in a terrible mess. But he was making an enormous lot of money. Instead of reporting the situation to my superiors, I decided to blackmail him.'

'You,' I cried. She put back her head and laughed.

'You *are* an innocent,' she said 'If I was an ugly old woman you wouldn't have been surprised.'

'I'm not an innocent,' I said, 'and if you were an ugly old woman I wouldn't be sitting here talking to you. But what about Jackson? How did he react?'

'He didn't really mind a bit,' said Lena. 'In fact he respected me for it. It even excited his libido and he started chasing me all over the establishment and eventually I went to bed with him. Then I increased the blackmail and we became good friends. Actually I'm very useful to him because I'm extremely practical. I could have gone far in Inland Revenue, but the truth is that I only excel in fairly desperate conditions. I would have made a good soldier.'

Three

I met Inspector Gladcliff at Jackson's establishment. He was a shortish, middle-aged man with a glass eye, the result of an injury he had received during the last war, and was restless, talkative and aggressive in manner. In order to have a satisfactory conversation with him, you had to watch each eye separately and mentally compare notes. I discovered that he was more or less permanently attached to Jackson's establishment. 'I never make any arrests,' he said.

'Then why are you here?'

'As a liaison officer of sorts,' he said, 'to see everything in order. I like neatness above everything else, that's why I joined the force.' It immediately crossed my mind that Gladcliff was blackmailing Jackson, but I decided not to ask him.

'I'll tell you what it is,' said Gladcliff. 'You've got to make allowances. Take the police force. We're not here to abolish murder or larceny or adultery or pornography; on the contrary we welcome it—there's a lot to be said for drugs and obscenity, and, whatever people may think, we have no time for the Church. They are supposed to have invented virtue, but I've yet to discover it. No, the point is, you've got to be sensible. You can't dodge the parade. A bit of bull, tidying-up, a good smashing salute, God Bless the Queen, and then let Hell loose.'

'That's an admission,' I said.

'It's a fact,' said the Inspector, 'It's a vital fact. For instance, you've got to keep the myth going about people being good, particularly people in important positions, but you've also got to allow quite a lot of people to be bad. The big question is, who are allowed to be bad? That's where we come in.'

'Would I be allowed to be bad?' I asked.

'It could depend on your bank balance and your war record,' said the Inspector.

'And Jackson?'

'Definitely,' said the Inspector. 'He's well inside what we call the "Reservation" or, at other times, the "Club." The Reservation also includes Members of Parliament, the Cabinet, all Forces ranks above captain, the Royal Family and quite a sprinkling of portrait painters. We don't allow them to crack their image, the Image that must, above everything, be kept.'

'That's very old-fashioned,' I said, 'and not entirely true. What about Profumo?'

'Stupidity is worse than vice,' said Gladcliff. 'Let's not talk about that. Our only real trouble is the Young.'

'In what way?' I asked.

'They don't run true to form,' said the Inspector. 'They're the greatest problem this country—and even the whole Free World—has to face. In the old days we could keep a tab on them. A great many of them were underfed, they fitted neatly into Borstals and approved schools, the Boy Scout movement was flourishing, there were boys' clubs and boys' brigades, and you could shoot them into the Navy and the Army. You could make men of them. Look at the wars. And the Church can't do anything with them.'

'I thought you weren't interested in the Church,' I said.

'A good strong church is the only thing for Youth. Christ is the best example for them. As long as they keep away from Mary Magdalen,' said Gladcliff. 'They've got to be organised.'

'You mean there's a complete break,' I said.

'A complete break,' said Gladcliff. 'There's no such connection between us and them. Even games aren't giving them any discipline.'

'But what's wrong with them?' I asked.

'It's difficult to say,' said the Inspector. 'It's like a different race. You can't trap them any more. Not with the old tricks, straight shoulder-to-shoulder talk, advice about girls, not even art like Beethoven or Elgar. Beethoven and violins and Rupert Brooke, they were grand for youth who didn't kick footballs about. No, they have invented something. They have invented something miserable and marvellous like children abandoned on an island. Like people from the moon. We've got to break it.'

'It's war,' I said.

'It's war,' said the Inspector.

'It's a horrible war,' I said. 'A war between the Old and the Young.'

'It's a horrible war,' said the Inspector, 'but it's well planned. We're starting with flattery, we soften them up and then we hand them over to the generals and the bishops for a grand universal crucifixion.' He took out a cigarette and lit it. 'Not that I don't like young people,' he said.

I would have given my views, but decided against it. 'I want to talk to you about Jackson,' I said.

'What about Jackson?' asked Gladcliff sharply.

'It's this business about "Bugs" Norton,' I said.

' "Bugs" Norton,' said the Inspector. 'What's wrong about him? Good fellow, a bit touchy, one of us. He runs the Stepney gang.'

A new orchestra came up on to the stage of the nightclub. There was a tickle of marimbas, a cough of Congo

24

drums and then a faintly suburban edition of a rumba permuted into the softly-lit room. I recognised the band. It had played from Mayfair into the television screens for apparent ages. It was supposedly Latin American, but it was merely the breath of Victor Silvester tinged with very faint garlic.

'You know Jackson is going to kill "Bugs" Norton,' I said.

'Jackson tell you?' asked Gladcliff.

'Yes,' I said. 'What are you going to do about it?' I asked.

'Nothing,' said Gladcliff. 'Why should I? It's all in order, it would be like stopping a boxing match. Norton's establishment is inside the Reservation, like this one and a hundred others. The rules are primitive, I grant you, but we're not against fresh air among paid members. Besides we've got to have something to show foreign V.I.P's apart from the Houses of Parliament, the Changing of the Guard and the Festival Hall.' He gave me a huge clap on the back and ordered another brandy.

"I refuse to have anything to do with this,' said Doctor Swinger, 'either medically or from a psycho-neurotic standpoint. I absolutely refuse.'

'Then you are the accomplice of a murder,' I said, 'and even more than that, you refuse to examine a man who has recently changed his identity, and discovers himself in a situation beyond his control, which leads to this murder.'

'Absolute poppycock,' said Doctor Swinger. 'Half-baked science fiction. My profession consists of listening to fantasies and diverting them back to reality and its components, not the other way round.'

I had obtained an introduction to Doctor Swinger from a friend of mine who was a publisher. I had told this publisher that I wanted to write an article about psychiatry in the modern scene, and in this guise I had gained entry into Doctor Swinger's office. The Doctor had red hair and a face that seemed to have been hastily put together at the foot of a sharp, questing and angry nose.

'You writers are a great trouble,' said Doctor Swinger, 'because you are all apologetic misfits. Anyone, absolutely anyone in the world knows more about reality than you do.' He pointed dramatically out of the window. 'Say that man in the garage opposite in overalls. Or the policeman coming up the road. Their reality quotient is ten times higher than any of yours. The only way you get by is to discover something which everybody knows and purvey it to people who are trying to forget.'

'What's that?' I asked.

'Death,' said Doctor Swinger. 'Decomposition and despair. The more ingenuous you appear to be in your discoveries, the more success you achieve, because the so-called commercial benefits thrust on to the civilised world preach complacency and good cheer.

'I am not speaking about the secret alleyways of love——whatever that is—because they are more dangerous than any forms of honest egotism. Divert love.' His face leant forward suddenly and his nose bleakly gleamed like a dead fish. I began to get bored. This mangled speech of his not only had nothing to do with the predicaments of Jackson and Gold and the death of Norton, but gave me the impression that the man was mad. Even though it is fairly widely known that most psychiatrists are mad, and that they use their profession as a form of jargon-filled auto-therapy, I also felt that Dr Swinger was playing some sort of part, and that he was not telling the truth.

26

'You ask me to listen to this cock-and-bull story,' continued the Doctor, 'and then behave like a correspondent for *Psychic News* or the Vice President of the Flying Saucer Society. With all this suffering in which we are immersed. The global starvation, disease, persecution and endless permutations of despair which govern the human race, topped by a seedy sugar icing of speculators, pools winners, ruthless top ten neurotic idols, faceless actors and drunken over-paid reporters. Forget the streamlined intellectuals, they're all tuft hunters.

'How many times have I been crucified?' cried Doctor Swinger.

'I've no idea,' I said, stifling a yawn.

'Ten, fifteen, twenty times,' he said. 'Each time I have dropped off my cross, crawled away and my wounds have been licked by pariah dogs, nymphomaniacs and fashionable doctors. I have gone mad a score of times, screaming, flat as a worm, on the ground and then, in silence, I have heard the birds singing like I did when I was a child. But I never surrendered. I insulted everybody at cocktail parties until I discovered the occasional Christ, the man at the back door.'

'What are you trying to say?' I cried with sudden anger. I had presented him with a phenomenon and the best he could do was to whine about himself. 'Does everyone change their identities all the time?' I asked.

'It's not important,' said the Doctor. 'It's not relevant to anything that matters. Miracles or scientific sensations, dubious acts of physical or psychological exploration, sagas of spiritual endeavour, they're all of no importance whatever. There's only one thing that counts, only one thing which keeps me riveted to my profession.'

27

'What is that?' I asked wearily. Perhaps it is impossible to talk to anyone objectively, we are all embedded with the barnacles of obsession, disease, guilt and flickering hope which make it impossible to conduct any reasonable conversation for longer than a minute.

'It's Luck,' said the Doctor. 'Luck and only Luck. Put it like this. Imagine an enormous mountain which is quite impassable. On one side of the mountain live the lucky. On the other side the unlucky. And there you are. Both sides have the same laws, food, chances, education, talent, stupidity, courage, beauty, ugliness and so on. It doesn't make any difference. It doesn't matter how evil, lazy or ignorant the lucky ones are, or how exemplary the unlucky. Life belongs to one, it is denied to the other.'

'That's a sort of Fascism,' I cried.

'Call it what you like,' said the Doctor. 'It's the only fact. You could say it was the only religion man has ever known. Suppose that a road was eventually constructed over the mountain so that one group could pass over to the other. There would be an intermingling, and then what would happen? The lucky side of the mountain would become the unlucky one, and vice versa.'

'It's an over-simplification,' I said. 'And, in any case, why should the lucky ones take over the other side of the mountain?'

'Because Bad Luck is infectious,' cried the Doctor, banging his fist on the table.

There were so many contradictions in the Doctor's speech that I didn't trouble to discuss the question with him. Also his questing, angry nose and shrouded eyes made me feel he was something worse than dishonest. 'I'm sorry you can't help,' I said, rose, and shook hands with him. I left his consulting room, opened the door and entered the waiting-room. There was only one man inside it, seated near a large mirror. I recognised him at once, or rather I recognised his face and appearance. It was Richard Gold. Richard Gold the Second. He looked at me distantly, and then nodded. He seemed almost to have forgotten that he had met me in his club.

Four

I had fallen asleep for a minute or two and turned my head around and saw Lena's head on the pillow. I stretched happily, kissed her, and gave her a cigarette and lit it. Then I lit a cigarette for myself. Lena looked at me and laughed. 'That wasn't a bad performance at all,' she said.

'Are you surprised?' I asked.

'Not intrinsically,' she said, 'but people hinted to me that you weren't any good in bed.'

'Dolts,' I said. I could see their white, race-card faces, I could see them shooting their cuffs over their Pimms Number One.

'There's no need to look bitter about it,' said Lena. 'I've told you it was a lovely performance. A brilliant first night.'

'It may get good reviews,' I said, 'but it won't be a long run.' Lena laughed and stroked my head.

'Don't worry about that. We can always change bits of

the play as we go along. It's the inner truth that counts. The bell rings and the house is safe.' I didn't say anything but stared at the ceiling.

'I'm a sensation seeker,' I said.

'People are only unhappy about love,' said Lena, 'because they've been taught that love isn't supposed to make you happy. There's an image of an unknown English gentleman who has made strict laws about love-making so as to get the least pleasure out of it and keep the individual personality un-stained by lust. That's why all Englishmen make love like Rudyard Kipling.'

'It's self-consciousness,' I said. 'The English have it like a disease. When you read the newspapers it is always Them to whom the dreadful things are happening, it is always They who do sordid things in Maidenhead. The English "I" is a perpetual island of virginity surrounded by himself.'

'No Englishman should be allowed to read his own lang-uage until he is thirty,' said Lena. 'He should be made to grope.'

'Groping in this climate can become a dangerous habit,' I said with some bitterness. 'You choke for air and become the slave of a slave.'

'Let's grope,' suggested Lena, sitting up in bed. She. . . .

CENSORED

'. . . as good as going to the Bahamas on a cattle-boat,' said Lena, lighting another cigarette and throwing a pillow at me.

'Could you tell me about Jackson?' I asked.

'What about Jackson?' said Lena.

'I mean, how is he behaving?'

'Frankly I can't make him out,' she said. 'He has become timid, gentle and thoughtful, like a floor-walker who's afraid of getting the sack. And there's something else about him which frightens me.

'It happened two nights ago,' continued Lena. 'It was about midnight. I was lying on the bed beside him and we were talking about "Bugs" Norton. He was asking me how he should kill him. Should he kill him with a knife or a gun or bang him over the head with an iron instrument? Or there was poison or fire or running him over. He seemed very precise about this, he appeared to want to do the right thing. He was talking like a gentleman, a rare enough thing nowadays, and certainly the last thing you'd associate with Jackson. I was pretty disgusted, I might tell you, because I can't stand gentlemen at any price. Up to now Jackson would have done anything at all without discussions or *thinking*. I remember the time he drowned a man in his bath, shaved at the wash-basin, and then calmly rang for the fire brigade.'

'He didn't waste time,' I said, kissing her ankle.

'Certainly not,' said Lena. 'I don't say he's terribly clever, but he's not cluttered up. At least, not up till now.'

'What happened then?' I asked.

'He suddenly fell asleep,' said Lena, 'and then this strange thing happened. The lamp at the bedside flickered and seemed to go sort of hard, operating-theatre colour. Then there was a strong smell of something like seaweed and smoke. It was the sort of smoke I had only smelt once before, in the early morning on the West coast of Ireland. It had made me think of the Fairies, you know, those people just round the corner.

The idea of them had always frightened me. They're Bad Luck.'

'What happened then?' I asked.

'The light seemed to get darker,' said Lena, 'and I thought I could hear the sea. Like a storm over the sea. In the middle of it there was a cry, but it wasn't human.'

'So what did you do?' I asked.

'I ran out of the room and went down to the Way Out Club and drank four large brandies,' she said. 'I hate the non-human. I hate wild animals and God and abstract paintings. People are cosy.' I thought about this, but didn't answer. Possibly stars do operate men. I had a longing to tell Lena about Jackson and Gold but decided against it. You can't talk to women about those sort of things, they don't merely think it ridiculous, it gives them positive pain.

'What happened then?'

'Inspector Gladcliff dropped in and we had another drink, and I began to feel a bit better.'

'What was he up to?'

'The usual business,' said Lena. 'Checking up on the business, looking out for the odd social agitator, Communist, non-accredited journalist or over-zealous policeman. He was asking me about a rather difficult bishop who apparently believes in emotional Socialism, when something odd happened.'

'What?' I asked half an hour later. 'A man came into the club, walked over to the bar and ordered a drink. He was a thinnish man, fairly personable, and dressed very neatly. He looked like some kind of minor official. He looked at the Inspector in a very sharp sort of way and then he looked at me and turned back towards Charles, the barman. Quite quietly he told Charles that his white coat was dirty and to change it at once. Then he started whispering to him and I

32

could see Charles go suddenly white. Charles disappeared from behind the counter and returned in a spotless coat and served the official another drink.

'That wasn't all,' continued Lena. 'When the official had finished his drink he turned back in our direction and beckoned towards the Inspector. It was a kind of imperious gesture quite unsuited to the appearance of the man. I am fairly quick at judging a man by his looks, I can X-ray his bank balance and his weaknesses like a flash, and I could have sworn to it that this official, or whoever he was, was essentially a tame man, an industrious man with all his papers in order. The sort of man who kept his mad dreams safely locked up from prying eyes, always put his coat on a coat hanger and folded his newspaper in exact rectangles. You know the sort of man I mean. The Nazis were like that, army officers are like that, bird-watchers and schoolmasters are like that. So are murderers.

'In any case, Inspector Gladcliff looked very surprised and walked over to him and asked him what he wanted. Then the official got very close to the Inspector and began whispering. Can you imagine my surprise when Gladcliff, in exactly the same way as the barman, went as white as a piece of paper and put his hand on the bar-counter to steady himself.

The official went on whispering, and then I distinctly saw the Inspector take a large sheaf of notes from his wallet and hand them over to the official. The Inspector looked really ill, and I must say I despised him.' And I despise you, I thought, looking at Lena, because I really dislike hard women. They can be marvellous momentarily, but their metallic competitive core turns life into a bloodthirsty kind of crossword puzzle without even a breather for a mild laugh.

'What happened then?' I asked.

'This official left,' said Lena. 'I turned to the Inspector with amazement. I asked him who this smarmy fellow was. He didn't answer for some time, he just drank glass after glass of whisky. Then he said he didn't know who the damned man was, but that the chap knew everything. He repeated "everything" three or four times. He was in a terrible state. He said he'd never known anything like it, and that the situation was damnably dangerous.'

'Dangerous to what?' I asked.

'You know,' said Lena. 'Our set-up. The organisation, or whatever you like to call it. The Forties Protection Society, because that's what we are. Noël Coward, Gathering Lilacs in the Spring again, drunken poets who were friends of Dylan, Spanish Civil War ex-generals who drink in the Antelope, four star perversions in small smart hotels with wishing wells, democracy with the best kind of cads in Wheelers, and reading *The Black Book* with a Nuits St. Georges 1929.'

'But you're too young for all that,' I said.

'It keeps me,' said Lena, 'and what keeps you makes you.'

I was certain that the 'official' whom Lena had described as having entered the Way Out Club was Gold. Gold-Jackson. My curiosity was now thoroughly aroused and I went to see Jackson the next morning in his office. He looked very old and mechanically handed me a cigar as though it was a ritual of self-preservation. 'I'm feeling my way around,' said Jackson, puckering his ugly, pugnacious face. 'I'm gradually discovering the people who are blackmailing me and the others whom I'm blackmailing myself. I can't say I wouldn't like to be out of the whole business, but if I tried another magical experiment God knows where I might land up. It could be a lot worse than this. You see, I've discovered that I'm really extremely rich, and I can't pretend that it hasn't had an effect on me. You actually and suddenly *own* money, like a starving man stumbling over a golden nugget, you want to hang on to it very tenaciously. It begins to own you. But I must say, I wish I didn't look like this.'

'You'll get used to it,' I said enviously. At that moment my attitude to Jackson changed, new, acquisitive, unspecified plans took its place. When Jackson had been Gold he hadn't possessed an enormous nugget.

'What have you discovered about your entourage?' I asked him.

'Well,' said Jackson. 'There's my wife, Phyllis. Apparently she's very rich, too. She's dull and plain and has a terrible shrill voice, and she spends most of her time singing at the grand piano in our apartment. Verdi, Puccini, and that sort of thing. Apparently somebody once told her that she should sing in opera, and that started it off and she's kept going by lots of odd people her husband has arranged for her. There's even a tame kind of Covent Garden impresario who appears overcome with emotion every time she hits a wrong note I don't altogether understand it, but I suppose I'll get around to it some time or other.

'Then there's this Bishop of Burnham Beeches who seems to have a lot of influence everywhere. I'm paying him regular sums of money for what appears to be unofficial advertisement in the proper quarters. He's supposed to be a great life-lover, and you can hear him booming with laughter two or three streets away, but the girls in my establishment don't like him at all, they say he's miserable and mean. He's Vice President of the Christian Rebirth Society, which has split off into two separate groups—possibly you've heard of them. One is the Trad. Business man Christ group, and the other is the Pop group, represented by a lot of younger types of vicars who go round on motor-cycles and throw custard pies at the church halls. I'm told they even "shake"—isn't that old-fashioned? But they're all the same at heart. I've met a psychiatrist chap called Dr Swinger, and he said they've all by-passed something. Not necessarily sex, but something like sex.'

'Who else?' I asked.

'There's Lena,' said Jackson. 'I expect you've met her.'

'Yes, I've met her,' I said. 'What about her?'

'She's amusing,' said Jackson, 'but I'm well aware that she's eventually going to betray me to Inland Revenue. But maybe that's a way out. Inspector Gladcliff knows a very important Commissioner who could be profitably introduced to the establishment. I'm aware that Gladcliff is only a sort of brutal sentimentalist, but I think he's on my side. If you know what I mean.' He poured out two glasses of whisky. 'The key man is someone called Jonathan Glory. Have you met him yet?'

'I've heard of him,' I said, 'and I've read him, but I haven't met him.'

'Then, as you know, he's the most famous columnist in the country, and even a richer man than me. Up to now I don't know very much about him, but I've heard that he's a very powerful manipulator indeed, the biggest "Communications" man in England, ranging from Buckingham Palace, the Houses of Parliament—any factions—the Archbishop of Canterbury, down to the distressed areas of South East Scotland. Nobody appears to know anything about his private life, but he's got tabs on everyone here. I'd like you to meet him.'

'I'm only an obscure writer,' I said. 'He wouldn't want to talk to me. Besides, I don't want to have anything to do with columnists.'

36

'That's sour grapes,' said Jackson. 'Worse still, it's lack of curiosity. That's your worst fault.' I was rather displeased by this statement and decided, nastily, to tell him about the latest development of his bi-cellular life.

'I've got news for you,' I said, swallowing the last of my whisky.

'What sort of news?' asked Jackson.

'Somebody called around here the other day,' I said.

'Anyone I know?' he asked.

'You don't know him,' I said maliciously. 'and he doesn't know you, but you have a lot in common.'

'I don't understand,' said Jackson ponderously.

'He was a man called Gold,' I said. Jackson stared at me for a full minute and then half-filled his glass with the rest of the whisky.

Five

'WHY don't you perform some of your magic properly?' I asked Jackson. He took a sip of his glass of stout and shook his head slowly.

'That's what people always say,' he said sullenly.

I had taken my friend to a pub well off the beat from Soho to have a good talk with him. This pub was called the 'Golden Lamb', tucked away in the brick wilderness of

Islington, a series of villages with odd timeless houses, hostelries and rituals tinged with ancient Cockney and Irish lore. Where else could you see the jig and the Hully Gully performed, simultaneously, by the old and young in tiny saloons flanked by beer barrels and brown ale, and where the hooded streets ring with vanished London cries of old iron, Jersey milk and Read All About It?

'But your point is,' I continued, 'that is to say, your magic point appears to state that the visible and the invisible can actually meet, and that a properly qualified magician can be a Lord of Creation. And just look at the mess you have made of it.'

'Knowing and doing are often separate things,' said Jackson.

'You have just contradicted yourself, then,' I said. 'Why can't you settle down and be a poet instead of turning into a gangster or an albatross? Yeats was a magician but he didn't try any of that nonsense. Quite apart from it being absurdly dangerous.'

'I was made that way,' said Jackson, ordering two more pints of stout. 'I was born believing in the gods, and not in God. That makes an enormous difference. I am not concerned with any sort of abstraction. I do not believe in trying to destroy evil or harp on what is called "good". I believe in what is in the wind, and it blows through people, mountains and rages through the stars.'

'You're a bloody Fascist,' I said, 'and you deserve your fate.'

'You're wrong,' said Jackson. 'You're damnably wrong. This thing is like light, it flickers and flares and fuses and you've got to learn all the laws to capture it. It is non-human, I grant you, but it is brighter than any of the distortions of Christianity.'

38

'What about "Regard the lilies of the field, they toil not, neither do they spin, yet Solomon in all his glory was not arrayed like one of these",' I said. 'Those are the words of Christ.'

'They could be the words of a drunken Persian poet,' said Jackson. 'Christ in an amalgam, the tragic story is crammed with the ideas of paralysed mountebanks. The only moving part of the half-fabricated story is his relationship with Mary Magdalen. Nobody ever discusses this. And nobody ever discusses the vile absurdity of his identification with the howling, blood-clotted masses. Had such an unlikely thing ever occurred, he would have bitterly regretted it.'

'Mary Magdalen,' I said, to elucidate that point.

'There was some truth in that,' said Jackson. 'In fact it's one of the only true things in the ridiculous story. This is the situation. Mary Magdalen. . . .

CENSORED

. . . . it leads to the desperate lack of happiness in this country, because Anglo-Saxons watch themselves being watched by everyone else, so that their identities are the result of a ballot, and nearly all their sub-conscious activities are a protest against this ballot.'

'That's all very fine,' I said, 'but what about the predicament you are in now?' I didn't tell him I was interested in his money even more than his predicament.

39

'What predicament?' asked Jackson.

'In the first place,' I said, 'there is this matter of killing "Bugs" Norton.'

'There's no trouble there,' said Jackson. 'It's a mere matter of procedure. You seem to forget I was in the army. I killed two men in Libya and another one in Holland. I used a hand-grenade in all three cases and finished them off with a bayonet. Half an hour later I was inspecting the company latrines.'

'Then there's Gold,' I said.

'He certainly is a bit of a problem,' said Jackson, 'because he's a licensed psychopath and the sort of dark horse I certainly wouldn't like to meet on a dingy night. I should imagine that he intends to take the Reservation over. Again, I mean.'

'So what do you propose to do?' I asked.

'Come to terms,' said Jackson. 'There's no other solution. But the situation has to be sounded out and I'm going to ask you to do the sounding-out for me.'

'I'm very busy,' I said untruthfully, 'and it might be dangerous.'

'I'll recompense you for your work,' said Jackson, staring down at the table, 'handsomely.'

'Very well, I'll do my best,' I said. 'How am I supposed to start?'

'With my wife, Stella,' said Jackson. 'Just feel your way along carefully and find out how the land lies.' He looked up at me with a hint of granite in his gaze. I felt a faint chill of amazement. There appeared to be little of the original, whimsical Gold left in his character.

I took a taxi to the Golds' house in Swiss Cottage and rang the bell. I had timed my visit with the hours of Gold's employment in the bank (providing he *was* working in the bank), and waited outside the door with more than the usual amount of nervousness which is associated with my character. Then I heard the approaching, muffled click of high heels, and the door was opened.

At first I could hardly recognise Stella. I thought I was confronting a sick middle-aged woman. She obviously had a black eye, which she had camouflaged with face powder. 'Anthony Carson,' she cried, and hesitated a moment or two. 'Please come inside and sit down. I will make some coffee.' I sat down in the lounge and stared edgily at the spot on the carpet where Richard Gold's straw bird used to be. Then I gazed at the walls and mechanically studied the pictures. They were all changed. Richard Gold (the First) had possessed a small collection of bird prints, the sort of delicate Audubon reproductions which you will find in the houses of quiet people, and he had decorated all the rooms of the flat with them, including the lavatory. Now, the wall directly in front of me was practically covered with photographs of strip-tease girls, dubious singers, boxers smiling out of their frames with the fake amiability which goes with possible contracts, and a hideous woman in a huge white hat who could have been somebody's mother. There was a large Toby jug on the mantelpiece and a box of half-finished cigars on a side table. The room smelt of tobacco, whisky and sour leather.

Stella came in and handed me a cup of coffee and put her own cup down on the table. She sat down and stared at the carpet. 'How is Richard?' I asked, trying to sound casual. There was a fairly long pause.

'I don't really know how to start,' she said in a tiny voice. 'The whole thing has been a bit of a shock.'

'What happened?' I said. 'It's Richard,' she said, looking

41

slowly up at me. 'He's taken to drink. It's not that I mind him taking to drink. On the contrary, I could be pleased, because it would mean it was taking his mind off that bloody, disembodied magic. It's the way he drinks that upsets me so much. He drinks like a car salesman and then he beats me up.'

'That's a bit much,' I said. Stella choked on a laugh. It was a bit forced.

'It isn't that I really mind being beaten up occasionally. All women rather love it. It's the way he beats me up. Terrible heavy breathing and unsteady battering. Then he gets sentimental and there are tears in his eyes. All that. It gets rather boring to say the least of it.' She looked down at the carpet again. I didn't know what to say. There was obviously a great deal I could say, but I didn't see that any point would be gained by explaining the truth of the situation, certainly not yet.

'It must be awful,' I said.

'Yes,' she said. 'I know I must look awful,' she continued and tried to laugh again. It was a sad attempt. I took her hand and squeezed it. 'And then there are the pictures on the walls,' she said. 'I suppose you've seen them.'

'I have,' I said. 'I was a bit surprised.'

'You should see the bedroom,' said Stella. 'The walls are plastered with them. It's not that I mind naked ladies, I can enjoy them almost as much as a man, and I have nothing against boxers, on the contrary I love bloodshed, but I don't like either of them simpering. Nakedness and punching are a serious business. There, I am talking too much!' But I could see she looked a little bit better.

'What about his work?' I asked, changing the subject.

'He goes to work just the same,' said Stella. 'He's terribly punctual, as a matter of fact, and I have the impression that he works harder than ever before. In fact he brings work back from the bank and spends hours adding up figures. You can hardly go into the room through the fog of cigar smoke and the fumes of whisky. I will say they're good cigars, though. I admire him for that.'

'It's something,' I said. 'Anything else odd about him?' Stella sat quietly for a minute or two thinking.

'There are two things,' she said slowly. 'The first one is that he has more power than before. A sort of lumbering power that I've never known him have. He has more power in his thumb, even when he's drunk, than he ever had, sober, in his whole body. It's not the sort of power I like, mind you, but it's there.'

'And the second thing?' I asked.

'It's something he said in the middle of the night. It was two or three days ago. I think he was asleep and he wouldn't have known I heard it. It was something about robbing the bank. And then he said the name "Jonathan Glory".'

Six

'I have a feeling,' Jackson told me, 'that my wife —I mean, of course, my new wife—suspects something about me. She looks at me in a very peculiar way. Not only that, but Inspector Gladcliff told me that somebody had told him that she'd been seen with "Bugs"

Norton. After all, he's my deadly enemy and she should be perfectly aware that I am going to kill him.'

'What do you propose to do about it?' I asked.

'I'm asking you to do something about it,' he said. 'I want you to get friendly with Phyllis and find out how the land's lying. You'll get on well with her because she admires writers and architects and portrait painters—provided they look moderately well off and don't become technical. She never reads anything, in fact, except the newspaper columns by Jonathan Glory, and most of them make her weep openly.'

'I'll have a shot,' I said and kept silent for a bit. I was thinking.

'What are you thinking about?' asked Jackson craftily. I looked into his eyes and felt quite shocked to observe how neatly he was settling down inside his new skin.

'I presume I am on expenses,' I said casually. Jackson stared up at the ceiling, then looked at me and away with the speed of a snake's tongue. 'You're on a salary,' he said, reaching for a sheet of paper. 'How about twenty a week?'

'Fifty a week,' I said, without hesitating.

'Have you ever mentioned anything of this affair to anyone?' he asked, putting his face closer to mine. His breath smelt of peppermint.

'I mentioned details of the phenomenon itself—after all, it's of scientific interest—but I didn't disclose any names.'

'Whom did you mention it to?' asked Jackson.

'A doctor,' I said, 'a sort of psychiatrist. His name's Swinger. A harmless sort of gasbag. He didn't believe me.'

'Swinger,' Jackson repeated. 'I know Swinger. He's been around here long before the change. He's a friend of Phyllis's, and you see him with all the boys. He's a top-level blackmailer. He does it for some sort of organisation. You certainly chose a winner there, Carson.'

'I did it for you,' I said. 'I wanted to stop you being killed.'

Jackson pulled out a box of cigars, snatched one of them out, crammed it into his mouth and lit it. The air tingled with Edwardian revelry. 'I don't like cigars,' he said suddenly. 'I don't like those boxers and naked ladies on the walls.' He blew out a balmy cannonade of smoke. 'All right, it's fifty,' he said harshly.

Later that evening I went round to the Reservation Club, the smart section of Jackson's establishment, and was shown to a table by myself. I ordered a private bottle of whisky and signed for it, something which gave me a momentary plea-sure, being the sort of writer I intrinsically am—as well as the writer I have turned out to be, a minimal sort of success-failure. I have occasionally found myself living like a temp-orary millionaire, regained some kind of inherent confidence, and then been thrown back on to the hard pavement of the non-conformist's alleyway, clinging on to good English but clutching the wrong flag, before and behind my time with a horizon of bars and fantasy.

A few tables away I could see Phyllis. She was dressed in a fruit-like dress, purple and over-ripe, and her face had an unhealthy blaze. Her husband, Jackson, was not there, but she was surrounded by a group of courtiers. Nearly all of them seemed, at first glance, crippled or deformed and two of them were agitated by the convulsions of Parkinson's disease. Each individual, except for a youngish man who was obviously blind, was well over the age of fifty. While I was inspecting the party, Inspector Gladcliff approached the table, bent over Phyllis Jackson's hand and ostentatiously kissed it. As he rose up his head turned in my direction and he appeared a little uncomfortable. He came over to me and sat down.

'You know Phyllis, don't you?' he asked. 'She's a marvellous woman. Fascinating and very witty. So rare these days.'

'I haven't met her,' I said. 'I've heard she's very rich.'

'That's possible,' said Gladcliff.

'Who are all her friends at the table?' I asked.

'Her permanent court,' said Gladcliff. 'Haven't you been told about it? It's been going on for years, ever since she was a girl, when Jackson and she were married. We call them the "chastity belt". Jackson, you see, has always been a teribly jealous man, and from the very beginning he started to encase his wife with a type of human bandage, consisting of the most innocuous, physically and mentally deficient, impotent group of men he could discover in London. Any man who approaches Phyllis with a gleam in his eye—which might seem difficult to imagine—generally disappears and is never seen again. At least three such individuals have been hauled out of the Thames, and the coroner always gives a verdict of unrequited love.'

'She seems as though she might be rather a dangerous kind of friend.' Gladcliff gave a short laugh.

'There's nothing for you to worry about,' he said. 'You look harmless enough.' I couldn't think of anything to say, so I laughed too.

I offered the Inspector some of my whisky, and we settled back in our chairs. 'Do you believe in magic?' I said, after a short silence. Gladcliff replied on the spot. 'No, I don't,' he said, 'but I know a hell of a lot who do and most of them are behind bars. All that lark is like drugs. Trying to take a short cut. One of my kids told me he saw a fairy in the garden

46

and I walloped his bottom so hard that he couldn't sit down for three weeks. I suppose you think I'm old-fashioned?'

'Possibly,' I said, swallowing some whisky.

As the Inspector stopped talking, a tall stout man entered the club. He had a port-and-sherry complexion, a large nose and a bulging forehead. He was very well dressed, almost foppishly, and his posture was bent, his eyes on the floor. He exuded a sort of softness, but it was the softness of a cactus with spines. He walked over to Phyllis's table and, in precisely the same manner as Gladcliff, kissed her hand, and nodded affably to the rest of the company. 'That's the only other man who can jolly up Phyllis,' said Gladcliff. 'The power of the Press.'

'Who is he?' I asked.

'That's our dear, beloved Jonathan Glory,' said the Inspector. 'The power behind the throne.'

'I never thought he looked like that,' I said. 'I imagined someone thin, pale and haggard.'

'Would you like to meet him?' asked the Inspector.

'He wouldn't want to meet me,' I said with an almost genteel, false humility. These days, to condemn a bad prose style combined with a large bank balance is a sign of madness. You have to be subtle to attack the top ten.

'He's not at all stuck up,' said Gladcliff. 'He stops and talks to everybody. He's interested in everything. That's his genius.' I curdled gently, but said nothing. Gladcliff waved towards Glory, who waved back and came towards us. He had eyes like an owl.

'Hullo, Great Chief,' said Glory, slapping the Inspector on the back.

'I want you to meet a great friend of Jackson's,' said Gladcliff, nodding his head towards me. 'His name is Anthony

Carson.' Glory suddenly sat down and peered at me. His complexion was rosy but not very healthy. There was a very slight twitch at the corner of his mouth, but you had to look hard to notice it. I wondered what it betrayed, but couldn't make up my mind.

'What sort of friend?' asked Glory, smiling. His open mouth looked like a hot oven. 'You don't look like a friend of Jackson's, you look like a season-ticket spectator.'

'He employs me,' I said, trying not to sound annoyed.

'Good God,' said Glory, and laughed. He had too many teeth altogether. I tried to remember those warm, chubby bits from his columns, like doorsteps so clean with detergent and tears that you could eat off them.

'I'm not blackmailing him,' I said, sounding through the fog. These words had no effect on him.

'Old Jackson's certainly got a bit queer lately,' said Glory. 'Do you know why?' He leant his face forward to me, and when I looked into his eyes I had the impression he knew, if not everything, something.

'I don't,' I said.

'It's a queer life,' said Glory. 'I was saying the same only yesterday to a man called Swinger. Have you ever met him?' Again his eyes tapped at me.

'Superficially,' I said.

'So you write,' said Glory.

'He makes things up,' said Gladcliff, laughing. 'Maps and things like that. I read one of his stories and it could never have happened. It was in Spain and I've been to Spain on business, and this wasn't Spain. Good luck to you.' He turned and patted me on the back. 'Jonathan writes about real people in real situations,' said the Inspector.

'I know,' I said. 'I haven't been able not to read them.'

48

'Good,' cried Glory. 'We'll all have a drink.' He ordered drinks and moved his chair nearer to me. 'To hell with writing,' he said. 'It's not a matter for discussion by gentlemen. Although, I would like to mention, as a sort of joke, that when I was a young man I wrote two plays in medieval Latin and they were both performed in Chichester. Beauty, wit and terror, my dear friend. Yes, yes. No, I want to know more about Jackson. Will you have lunch with me tomorrow?'

'I would like to,' I said.

'Good. After lunch, I go to work and I would be glad if you would accompany me on my rounds.'

'Yes,' I said, thinking—why not? There was no need for me to give anything away.

The orchestra had been playing a morsel from *My Fair Lady*, but it had now stopped, and the memory of the music hung in the air like a stale dream, and then blew away. The room was full of chattering, two world wars hadn't dented it, the tango was dying, Cockney accents stormed the clubs, but the dog was still king, Agatha Christie was Queen of the box-office, and the ageless homosexuals still decorated the nostalgic haunts. People were dying, old friends were wounded, drugged, there were a few suicides, they were just over the cosy horizon, somebody had written a book about Jack's cousin, it had been well reviewed by Bill, the old drunk.

Jackson came in, looked around the room and sat down at a table by himself. He looked all in. I watched his bloated face, and couldn't help thinking of the albatross winging the scuffed Atlantic in its slow, high dream. I laughed, stopped laughing and lit a cigarette. The music started playing again, then a saxophone choked on a note, spluttered, and there was silence. The whole room was silent. Nobody moved, but I could see people's eyes turned towards one of the doors, fixed. A man had entered the club and was slowly looking around the room. He was a very tall man, well dressed, with a beaked nose and a livid scar down one side of his cheek. He began to move, without haste, from table to table, until he stood in front of Phyllis Jackson and suddenly put his hand on her shoulder. The air sparkled with electricity, I wouldn't have been surprised by lightning and thunder. A waiter approached, and the tall stranger gestured for a chair. He sat down and took Phyllis's hand. He was master of the situation. He always had been.

' "Bugs" Norton,' whispered Jonathan Glory.

People's eyes now turned towards Jackson, with the expression, the certainty, the need of 'This is it'.

'This is it,' whispered Jonathan Glory, showing all his carnivorous teeth. But Jackson sat quietly at his table, drinking a glass of mineral water, and eating his own private thoughts. Everybody in the room was aware that a killing was on the cards, that it was Jackson's first move. It was a blood-letting within the Reservation circle, both of them had been asked to country houses, it was as good as hunting or adultery in the left wing. In fact, it was a sacrifice. But still Jackson didn't take any notice.

'Bad Theatre,' hissed Glory impatiently.

Only I, apparently knew the reason. It was simple enough. Jackson, though aware of the fact that he had to kill 'Bugs' Norton, had never known what he looked like. The man seated beside Phyllis, his wife, was merely a stranger. He continued to drink his mineral water.

'Jackson's a bloody coward,' said the Inspector in a fairly audible voice.

'That's right,' said a red-faced man at the next table. 'He's as yellow as a buttercup.' I got up from the table and crossed

50

the room to sit beside Jackson. It was loyalty to my employer. I had no intention of betraying the identity of Norton. I ordered a drink and asked him, 'What's wrong?'

'Lena's dead,' said Jackson.

'Dead,' I said. I hadn't seen her for two days. Then tension of the great, vindictive, extraordinary world had been greater than hers. My eyes were suddenly wet and I swallowed my glass of brandy.

'She was killed,' said Jackson. 'She was smashed to death in a wood on Hampstead Heath and her head was in a polythene bag. I've just heard it on the radio.' I felt sick. I thought that I understood what had happened. Somebody had guessed the truth. But it was no good to Jackson.

'Inspector Gladcliff will see everything's all right,' I said. 'There's nothing to worry about.'

Seven

JONATHAN GLORY'S house was off Regent's Park and when you climbed upstairs into the drawing room and looked out of the window there was an enormous stretch of country green and little blazes of flowers. If this was the reward for writing all that trash it certainly seemed worth while. It was a very large house in almost agonizingly good taste, not a single thing in it could be faulted by the Reservation magazines, it was even deliciously casual. I wasn't surprised to see a Picasso on one wall,

and a small Renoir on another, and there were a few Koko-
schkas and a Kandinsky. 'He's like a fountain, don't you
think?' said Glory. I could feel he didn't like me, I was right
out of it, but he was doing his best to humour me, and he
even referred to his house as a bit of a shack. I laughed at
this, perhaps a little servilely. I would let him pull my leg as
well as his own.

'We'll have a drink,' said Glory, going over to his bar. 'Do
you like Campari?'

'Very much,' I said.

'It should really only be drunk in hot weather,' said Glory,
but you can pretend. I'm drinking Passion Fruit—a bit suburban, I know—bacause of my afternoon's work. I'm very
strict about that. Not a smell on the breath.' Some other
guests arrived. There was the Bishop of Burnham Beeches, a
stout elderly cleric, and a young man called the Reverend
Roger Rout. The conversation succeeded in astounding me.
It was mostly about flogging and capital punishment and
praise for the police. There was an atmosphere of hatred and
fear and, more than that, contempt for the vast unacceptable
sea of humanity which washed up against their rigid, over-
insured dykes.

'You've got to trap them first,' said the Bishop.

'The Bishop is right,' said Roger Rout, whose thick horn-
rimmed glasses gave him an intellectual, modernist air.
'You've got to be very careful. You've got to get inside their
skins, you've got to be *like* them, otherwise they don't trust
you.'

'There's no need to tell me that,' said Glory, laughing.

'You're a marvellous actor,' said the Bishop, laughing as
well, 'but you're only touching a relatively small part of
them, notably the aged and people with arthritis.'

'And Bright's disease,' said Glory, sipping his Passion Fruit. 'I got a good Bright's disease last Friday on a council estate. Mrs Fisk, her name was.'

'And you're too moral, Jonathan,' said the Bishop. 'You're too *decent*, altogether too decent for the ones who are a bit more than half-educated, and there are quite a number, I'd say. You're "plugging", if you'll excuse the word, too much the British Legion and Dunkirk and people who've never seen a refrigerator. These people are dying, Glory, dying. It's the living we've got to wory about. All the way from China to Dagenham.'

'I expect Khrushchev has much the same trouble,' I said mainly because none of the three had been paying any attention to me. They turned their eyes on me in amazement, and then the Bishop nodded his head.

'That could well be true,' he said, and stared down at the floor. We walked into the dining-room and sat down to lunch. There was even a rosy-faced old butler with white hair, whom, I was told later, Glory had saved from alcoholic destitution and who, for this reason, received no pay.

Over scampi the argument about the great untidy world at their doors continued. They were all frightened of youth, but the Reverend Roger Rout was sure of his own plan. 'If we imitate youth, exactly imitate it, that's something. But if we forestall it, that's more effective still. As an example of the first, look at our success in completely cornering the entire Top Twenty three weeks running. Not a word about girls or Baby, all God and the Virgin Mary. We have three revues running in the West End, scooter rallies at Weston-super-Mare, and a cabaret with soft drinks in St. Paul's. But it's not enough. I propose we enter the satire market.'

'God forbid,' said the Bishop, looking at Glory.

'I suppose he's right,' said Glory without enthusiasm, 'but there are simpler ways than that. I've been speaking with the P.M. and he agrees with me. I suppose you think I'm old-fashioned, but the only thing is to manufacture a gigantic war-scare and get them all conscripted.'

'Get their God-forsaken hair cut,' cried the Bishop.

'Make them march until they drop,' said Glory. 'I was in the Army and it made a man of me.'

'In any case, something's got to be done,' said the Bishop, 'before they collar the universities and vote all of us out of the government.'

'Start with my plan, first,' said Rout. 'Soften them up and then get their guilt working.'

'Wouldn't it be even better,' I said, during a pause in the conversation, 'if you started off by really liking the revues and the pop-songs and the satire, and then had the satisfaction of honestly betraying them?' Again, they all looked at me in amazement and then Glory gave a short, rather nasty laugh.

'He's a clever fellow, Carson,' he said.

We returned to the drawing-room and drank coffee. I heard a bell ring downstairs and then the butler appeared and announced Mrs Phyllis Jackson. She was wearing a sort of striped dress which made me think of shop awnings and old-fashioned bathing tents, and ample as the material was, she still managed to bulge through it in rather unexpected places. Her face was white with powder, through which blazed two blue eyes of uncompromising candour, like a furious kitten. It was easy to see, even under the striped dress, that she was shaking all over. Glory rushed over to her and helped her collapse into an armchair.

'My dear Phyllis,' he cried, 'may I give you a drink?'

'A large brandy,' said Phyllis in a voice like a tiny scream. She drank it down in one gulp.

'Is something wrong, my dear Mrs Jackson?' asked the Bishop, moving towards her.

'You could say something is wrong,' said Mrs Jackson with the same bottled scream. 'I've been raped.' There was a long silence. I turned my eyes towards Glory and at the same moment he looked at me. We seemed to exchange a short message. It is, in fact, possible to exchange an unspoken message between two individuals, the content of which is not overtly understood but merely dimly felt. Such a message is docketed in some mysterious cupboard of the brain and never fades.

Nobody moved for quite a time. Then the Bishop coughed. 'Dear, oh dear,' he said in a low voice. He obviously wasn't good at life. He didn't even like talking about it directly, and later Glory told me that years ago a female cook had said something to him which had put him to bed for three weeks with a high temperature. He had deliberately forgotten what the cook said. It was something like those court cases, the sort of things *they* did.

'It's the shock,' said the young vicar, 'these sort of things can give one a shock.' Glory buried his face in hands and then looked up, red in the face. You could see all his teeth.

'Perhaps it would help settle you, settle you, if you told us what happened.'

'This man suddenly came into my bedroom,' said Phyllis, 'and got me by the throat.'

'Which man?' asked Glory. 'Could you describe him?'

'He was a youngish, slim kind of man,' said Phyllis, pulling at a strand of her purplish hair. 'He seemed to have a kind, trustworthy face. The sort of face I'd have asked the

55

way from. But he pushed me down on the bed and raped me.' Her bright blue eyes were suddenly bubbling with tears.

'It's never happened to me before. And from him.'

'What happened then?' asked the vicar. He seemed very interested.

'He made me get up off the bed,' said Phyllis, 'and go to the drawing-room and play the piano.'

'The piano,' cried the Bishop.

'Yes,' said Phyllis. 'I was trembling all over. He told me to play "One Fine Day". You know, the piece by Puccini. And he made me sing it. I had to sing it twice, and then he went away.'

'A maniac,' cried the Bishop. 'The whole country's full of them. If I had my way. . . .' I was conscious of Glory looking at me very intently, and I was certain that he knew something that nobody else knew. Except Swinger. I silently cursed myself for having confided, however vaguely, in that windbag.

'Now we'll have one more drink,' said Glory. 'It's a relief to get rid of those people. How I loathe, hate and despise people. Don't you?'

'I can't say I do,' I said. At times I did, but mostly I didn't.

'One only says one likes people to reassure oneself,' said Glory, 'because one daren't imagine that other people are the same as oneself.'

'I wouldn't like to dwell on that,' I said.

'I did,' said Glory. 'It suddenly happened to me when I was a young man at the university. It happened to me in a flash. I realised that I loathed the human race. I hated its preoccupations, it pretensions, its hidden vices. I hated its face. I hated the stupidity behind the beautiful face, the malignant

56

cunning behind the ugly one. I hated its culture. I hated its filthy, slobbering vugarity.'

'And you hated yourself,' I said.

'Certainly,' said Glory, laughing, 'but I was determined to be more than kind to myself. Jonathan Glory wasn't going to crucify himself for his discovery.' He laughed again.

'I am, of course, a popular columnist. You have, no doubt, perused my heart-throbs. You have sneered at them.' For answer, I smiled slightly. 'Exactly,' said Glory, 'and I am well aware that you have nothing but contempt for my prose style. Don't attempt to deny it. And I have an answer for you. I have a prose style, but I have no intention of having it contaminated by the eyes of the lower classes.'

'The lower classes?' I cried, astonished.

'Precisely,' said Glory. 'Not only the lower classes who sweat in their Bingo parlours, sing on street corners in their hideous raucous Anglo-Saxon voices, de-sex themselves at loutish football matches, picnic in murder gardens and read slavishly about upper-class orgies. Not only them, however much I despise them. Even more than that, I despise the lower classes who indulge in culture. The shark-like publishers dispensing Cadogan Gardens sex and Oxford Street whimsy. The literary "reviewers" filling in their forms for *Who's Who* and trying to invent ancestors who weren't slaves before the Repeal of the Corn Law. And the actors, my God, the actors, imitating all those accents and giving interviews every time they've gone to the lavatory. Need I go on.'

'No,' I said.

'I plump for the Aristocracy,' said Glory, after a moment's thought. 'You remember what Jesus Christ said. "They sow not, neither do they reap." Of course some of the bastards write, but they write so badly you readily forgive them, any sort of coronet is better coinage than the others.' Glory sipped his Passion Fruit and looked at me with something like candour. 'We, of course, both understand that there is only one permanence in existence.'

'And that?' I asked, half guessing what he would say.

'Magic,' said Glory, beaming. 'I'm sure you would agree about that. The indestructible. The eternally Modern. The *Satyricon* of Petronius. The *Golden Ass* of Apuleius. . . .' Glory seemed to be searching for a word, then he extended his large pink hands. 'The Albatross. . . .'

I didn't know what to say. Perhaps it was just a coincidence. perhaps it wasn't. It was impossible to tell, but I certainly wouldn't confide in him. 'I'll start work now,' said Glory, putting down his glass. 'I'll be down in a minute, if you don't mind waiting a bit.'

'Certainly,' I said. I drank my brandy slowly, thinking about the clue to existence. I could only believe in the horoscope of love. But I hadn't found it yet. Perhaps I was avoiding it. But I wouldn't choose the albatross.

A man entered the room silently. At first I didn't recognise him. He was wearing a cloth cap and an ill-fitting kind of hairy tweed suit and his legs were encased in gum-boots. The tie round his neck was in the style of a provincial undertaker. He came towards me and smiled, and I recognised Jonathan Glory. 'My working gear,' said Glory in a delighted voice. 'Don't you like it? A bit of everything for the proletariat. I think the tie is a particularly brilliant touch.'

'Splendid,' I said.

'It earns me thousands from the bastards,' said Glory.

'Congratulations,' I said as coldly as I could. I hated the way he talked about money.

'Then we'll start,' said Glory, taking out a briar pipe and

stuffing the bowl with tobacco. 'Merridew, that's my chauffeur, is waiting outside with the Rolls—I'm using the Phantom, because it's not so conspicuous. Then we'll roll along gently to one of the more depressing council estates—its called Beauty Grange—and I'll get down to the job. Come with me, of course.'

'I'd be very interested,' I said.

We went out into the street, entered the Rolls and drove off. After half an hour's driving we approached an area bristling with those sort of slabs of brick coloured heartbreak brown, which prick the London sky with a thrust of boredom and tears.

'Stop the car here, Merridew,' said Glory, pointing to a small, baffled square beside a neglected church and a betting shop. He put his hand on my arm. 'We'll walk from here,' he said.

'My dear Mrs Thrush,' said Glory, taking off his cap and bending over the chipped sink in the minute kitchen. 'How can you possibly cope with a sink like this? It is unspeakable. It is bad enough about the rats and the sludge in the cellar.' Mrs Thrush, a thin, elderly, bent woman with grey hair, was crying steadily in a corner of the room, under a stopped clock, the sort of clock that might have come from a Continental coach trip. To my amazement, Glory started crying too. I examined his face with care, and there were genuine tears rolling down his face. Suddenly he bounded across and grasped her hand. 'Mrs Thrush,' he said, chokingly, 'this is not the end of it. The tears in your poor, dear little kitchen will not be wasted. Your good, honest efforts will not be unsung. I, Jonathan Glory, will see to that. I would not fail you. Never, never would I fail you.'

'I know that, Mr Glory,' said Mrs Thrush, between her sobs. ' I have read you many times in *Women's Dreams* and I know the great heart you have given all such women as me, with no people or things to protect them.'

'That's right,' cried Glory, beating his thigh.

'Just one other thing, my dear Mrs Thrush,' said Glory, his eyes piercing hers. 'How often does your husband actually beat you?'

'At least four times a week,' said Mrs Thrush, bending over like an autumn leaf.

'You are a good woman,' cried Glory, seizing her hand again, 'and your goodness is like the goodness of our Saviour, Jesus Christ.'

'Amen,' said Mrs Thrush. There was a small silence. 'Would you gentlemen like a cup of tea?'

Glory and I visited about twenty tenants of Beauty Grange. With unerring instinct, Glory ferreted out the crippled, the diseased and the forsaken. His behaviour was impeccable, gentle, devoted and saint-like. It was impossible to fault him. I even found it difficult not to admire him for his professional expertise.

When, at last, we left the first three council houses and stood outside in the anaemic forecourts, where even the flowers were desperately trying to be sick, Glory took hold of my arm and pointed further along the block. 'One more person to see,' he said, with a smile. 'Just one more. But most important, for your sake as well as mine.' Gripping my arm a little tighter— and he was very muscular—he guided me towards Block E, which was also designated 'Gardenia Mansion'.

'It's on the third floor,' said Glory, 'and we'll walk up very slowly on, on account of your asthma.'

'Thank you,' I said.

We arrived on the third floor and stood outside a grey door from which the paint was peeling. 'I have the key,' said Glory, producing a bunch from his pocket and selecting one. He inserted it in the keyhole and we walked into a small flat almost devoid of furniture. The floor was littered with newspapers and there was a smell of something like bad fish. On a table in the corner with a broken leg was a book. I leant over and inspected it. It was Burke's Peerage, 1956. 'In the bedroom,' said Glory, opening another door. I followed him inside. There were more newspapers on the floor and a framed photograph on the wall. The photograph was of a dog, a sort of sad-looking Airedale, and there was something scrawled in ink on the bottom left-hand corner which looked like 'Love from Gruffy'. 'He loved dogs,' said Glory. There was a bed under the window and there was something like a skeleton lying on the bed half-covered by incredibly dirty sheets. I moved close, filled with so much nausea that I was fighting back the vomit, and fear lunged enormously into the room. It wasn't a skeleton, I could see, but a living man with a face as cracked, worn and yellow as an old cabbage leaf.

'You all right, Happy?' said Glory with a pleasant smile. He didn't answer, you couldn't even hear him breathing. 'Poor old Happy's resting,' said Glory. 'He's paralysed. Thinking of the old days.'

'The old days,' I said, trying not to look at Glory's atrocious, good-time grin.

'Six years ago he was boss of the "Reservation",' said Glory. 'Great friend of the Bishop of Burnham Beeches, and Inspector Gladcliff thought the world of him. So did I, for that matter. Unfortunately he slipped up.' He walked over and opened the bedroom window, breathing in the relatively fresh air. 'Had an accident,' said Glory in a loud voice which filled the room.

'Now work's over,' said Glory, when we had returned to his house. 'We'll both do some sensible drinking.' He walked over to the bar and returned with two large glasses of brandy and soda. Then he sat down and tapped me gently on the knee. 'You may or may not be a writer shimmering in a haze of pearly unrequited prose,' he said, but I am well aware that you are not earning the reward which is surely due to you. In that matter, if you will allow, I can help.'

'What am I supposed to do?' I asked, not looking at him.

'Tell me about Jackson and the Albatross,' said Glory. 'I have a completely open mind.'

Eight

When we kiss like this
I'm you, you're me
The moonlight that I see
Is the moonlight that you see
  The music and the flowers
    Are ours
    Eternally.

THANK God, I thought, this trivial little jukebox song isn't one of the religious ones which are beginning to crowd the Top Twenty and which, for all I knew, were being organised by

the Reverend Roger Rout to suffocate the hard-dying libidin-
ous themes. The singer had a slight touch of adenoids which
made the song quite affecting and sweet and blurred any
smart, glossy sign of the professional balladeer. I thought of
Lena, and there was a faraway pang of perfume and nearness,
and the long road of sadness which always follows life along.
Why was my life so episodic? Here I was, torn between
life and imagination, shy, gregarious with alcohol, trying
to check the undoubted laws of fantasy by the chaotic graphs
of human behaviour, putting my ear to the ground. Very
little conversation was of any value, the air was full of
diesel gas and class clichés and nobody grew flowers any
more.

> When we cling so close
> I'm you, you're me
> This ecstasy I feel
> Is the ecstasy you feel
> > These minutes and these hours
> > Are yours
> > Eternally.

Yes, it was a bit square, possibly, but at the same time it
was *fixed*, as they said in the modern language, it wasn't
stolen. It was a *neat fix*. I rather liked it, the old part of me
and the young part of me. Then somebody entered the club.
It was a woman who could have been twenty-five or thirty
(or more, but certainly not less). She was tall, with a slight,
gracious kind of stoop and long, not overtidy, blonde hair
which almost hedged her face. In fact she seemed to be using
this fairy-like hair as a curtain, through which she could
peep at the world without being discovered. She made me
think of a woodland animal, up and about at dusk among

63

the long grass, and you had to watch her very carefully, to pretend you weren't actually looking in her direction, to catch a glimpse of her face. This I at last managed, and received that sort of almost painful shock which only comes from the sudden impact of pure beauty.

> *As time goes by we'll go our different ways*
> *Troubles and tears will tempt us to forget*
> *But through the haze of all our darkest days*
> *We will remember yet. . . .*

She was shy, certainly, she was innocent, certainly, but there was also a flash of fierceness and perverseness in her lovely eyes, there was a hint of storms and swords that could kill, burn and destroy. She was dressed, not merely simply, but like a village girl. You thought of a sunshine salad, a tomato blouse, a lettuce skirt, cream shoes. She was utterly self-contained, the queen of no problems. 'It's a nice tune,' I said to the hair, as casually as I could. There was no movement, and then she looked at me and away again into the long grass.

'It's quite a nice tune,' she said, and suddenly laughed. I was surprised by the laugh, it was almost ugly, but it was very attractive, it was a bit the jeer of the village girl who is not quite laughing at the right things.

> *When a blackbird sings*
> *I'm you, you're me*
> *The road I'm walking on*
> *Is the road you're walking on*
> > *The sunshine and the showers*
> > *Are yours*
> > *Eternally.*

64

'Do you think it's a funny song?' I said, put out.

'No,' said the woman. 'I love those sort of songs which are old-fashioned.' And she laughed again, stopped, and looked at me quite hard. It wasn't a provocative look, or a particular kind of signal, but my nerves tingled.

'Do you work here?' she asked.

'I suppose I do, in a sense,' I said, 'though I mostly sit about and listen to the songs. As a matter of fact, I've never seen you in the Reservation before.'

'It's my first time,' she said in a soft voice. I felt we were back in the dusk again, and wanted to rustle the bracken.

'May I ask you your name?' She laughed once more.

'I'm laughing,' she said, 'because of the way you said that. About my name. Like some very important door-keeper. Do you mean my last name or my Christian name or my whole name? I'm called Penelope Lingley. I live in Devonshire, which is the best county, it's almost like living abroad. Will that do?'

'My name is Anthony Carson,' I said. 'I am a writer and ... well, I needn't go on.'

'Have you an inferiority complex?' asked Penelope. 'No, that's rude. I'm sorry. I didn't want to be rude. But I hate little people.'

'I'm not one,' I said. 'I'm as shy as you are, I suppose, until I start boasting.'

'There you are, we're quarrelling,' said Penelope, showing her very pretty white teeth with delight.

'Are you accompanied?' I asked.

'Vaguely,' she said, brushing aside her hair with her hand. 'Jonathan Glory has brought me here,' she said. 'Do you know him?'

'I know him slightly,' I said.

'Do you like him?'

'Not much,' I said.

'I expect you resent it that he's so successful,' said Penelope, laughing in that light, owl-sharp way which went so strangely with her beauty. 'But, in that case,' she went on, 'I don't think he's attractive or anything like that. He's amusing though. He brought me here to see the murder.'

'The murder?' I said, astounded, although I knew well enough what she meant. She could only be referring to the duel between Jackson and 'Bugs' Norton. Today was the day, and it had been industriously stage-managed, the theatre had been set, and the victim had been lured to his pre-destined spot.

'You have specially come here to see the murder?' I asked Penelope.

'Why not?' she said simply. 'I hardly ever go to the theatre and I don't read the papers, and I hate television. Mostly I live a very quiet life in the country. I suppose you think I'm very eighteenth century.' She turned her face full towards me and it blazed like a July garden, her mouth full as strawberries but shaped to a design of ageless loveliness. Was there amethyst and emeralds as well as summer sky in her eyes? Suddenly I felt engulfed, a huge wave knocked me down and I was struggling under a deep surge of water. I was utterly and desperately in love. Penelope.

'Why are you looking at me like that?' she asked. 'Don't you feel well?'

'It is your face,' I said in a stumbling voice. She frowned and was back in the wood.

'I hate people who look at me like a dog,' she said.

'I'm sorry,' I said.

'And I hate people who are sorry,' she said. 'And you're

more than a bit ruined. You must have been quite nice once, though.'

'That's something,' I said.

'It's not enough for me,' she said, 'at least I don't think so.'

'This thing just happened to me,' I said quickly. 'It just happened like a flash of lightning. I'm not trying to be romantic or sentimental or pathetic,' I said, not daring to even look in her direction.

'I know about my age and all the rest of it. . . ."

'Don't run yourself down so desperately,' she said. 'We don't know each other. You're moving with such terrific speed, it makes me dizzy.' She was still entrenched behind her hair, but suddenly, without being able to help myself, I ran towards her, put my arms on her shoulders and fingered aside her fairy hair and found her mouth on mine. I do not know how long it lasted, it may have only been a second, she pushed me away and I sat down, in a state that was terrible and marvellous at the same time. This was magic, the crystalline thing that was both experience and outside experience, all the women I had ever known in my life, all the places I had seen, faded into absolute nothingness and I was as happy and unhappy as I had never been before.

Penelope sat quite still, and I didn't know if she was angry.

'How boring,' she said in a tiny voice. 'Need everybody start fumbling at me just when I'm trying to be peaceful?' I felt wretched. Then she touched my hand. 'I'm sorry,' she said. 'I didn't mean that, you couldn't help it. At least I like to think you couldn't help it. It's a great compliment, I know.'

'May I see you again?' I cried in a voice that must have sounded absurd.

'Perhaps,' she said, and then laughed that adorable, ex-

67

asperating laugh. 'You really are awfully absurd. Like someone in the wrong play.'

At that moment, in this period of glorious misery, someone
entered the club. It was Jackson. Obviously he was looking for
me, but when he saw me seated close beside Penelope, he hesitated. Penelope, unexpectedly flung aside her hair and looked
directly at him. He, too, looked directly at her, and stood
motionless. It was, then, the look on his face that disturbed
me, an expression I had never associated with him before. It
was a frozen look, as though his life had stopped. He moved
forward a couple of steps and then stayed still, still staring
straight into Penelope's eyes. I suddenly wanted to hit him,
which was the very last sort of emotion I could have imag-
inged in relation to my friend, however changed his appearance. It is a more or less impossible feat to 'read' people's
thoughts, but there can be moments of awareness of psychic
states, general and particular, and the attitude of Jackson was
fairly clear to me. It was almost a conversation.

'This is Mr Jackson,' I said to Penelope.

'I have heard of you,' she said. 'You are famous. Particularly
today.'

'Oh, that,' said Jackson.

'I have been explaining to Mr Carson that I have come
especially from Devon to see the show.'

'It's a lot of fuss about nothing, really,' said Jackson. 'Let's
hope it's as good as the rehearsal.' All the time he never took
his eyes off Penelope, and I could feel the growing sparks of
hostility in the room. There was no doubt about it. Jackson
and I were suddenly enemies, all in the space of a few seconds,
because of a woman with long, fair hair in the corner of a
juke-box club.

'If it would be of any use to you,' said Jackson, uncertainly,

68

'you could use my office as a kind of a ring-side seat. It looks right down on the street where the action takes place.' He gave a short, rueful laugh.

'I'd love that,' said Penelope.

'I, myself, won't be present,' said Jackson. 'I'll be down on the stage, and I'll try to give you a good performance.' He seemed to leave the room very reluctantly.

'I love some sort of really ugly faces,' said Penelope, 'but the sort of men I generally end up with have rather sweet faces and are absurdly gentle.'

'Does that please you?' I asked.

'I am never satisfied,' she said, 'and I always do my best to try and change them. Their clothes, their shoes, their houses, their expressions. I wouldn't mind changing Jackson.'

'And me?' I asked. She looked at me seriously for a moment and then disappeared into the woodland.

'Bugs' Norton's impending death had been well publicised through the alleys, bars and clubs of Soho. It was also, obviously, well-known in Wapping and crowds of his supporters had moved into the area, headed by a small number of his lieutenants who were supposed to keep some law and order until the final solution of the problem. Naturally, the locality swarmed with police, nearly everyone of them disguised as layabouts, con-men and drug-pedlars, and so successful was this camouflage that the majority of the Law looked infinitely more criminal than the originals, and were studiously avoided by professionals, locals and tourists alike. All vantage points, even standing-room on the pavements, was portioned out by gang organisers, and itinerant street vendors were doing a brisk trade in tulips, roses, newspapers and copies of Old Moore's Almanac. They were even selling The War Cry.

But it was mostly a tourists' affair. The locals, the steady boozers and the Bohemian regulars were continuously bombarded by pistol shots, screams in the night, cries of rape, and they even stumbled over bodies as they staggered homewards at night, but they took no notice whatever. Soho is bound together by its own kind of psychic violence, the decks are cleared for a sort of grey, surgical gossip, people are murdered by words and discoveries, it is the most insular and the most British place in the world. But not to the tourist, the housewife from Penge, the couple from Cleethorpes, the business men's outing or the noisy colonials. For them Soho is a stepping-off place for the Continent, every sight, sound and smell is exquisitely Latin, everybody is licentious, romantic and gloriously depraved. It is an X film, in fact.

And somehow, the news of the murder had got through. Inspector Gladcliff had told me the news had been spread by the Soho shopkeepers' association on account of the benefits for trade, but it was also possible that the publicans had something to do with it. In any case, I had never seen the area so congested as I fought my way through the crowds towards the York Minster. Just outside the door of the public house I came face to face with Dr Swinger. 'The very man,' he said, without so much as a smile. 'I was on my way to see you at the Reservation. I want to talk to you. It's quite important.'

'Perhaps we could have a drink in here,' I said, pointing to the pub.

'I want to speak to you in private,' said the doctor.

'Very well,' I said, 'where?'

We took a taxi and went to his club, and entered a room where an old man was writing a letter at a desk far too small for him. I mentioned this to Swinger after we had sat down.

'He's writing to The Times,' said Swinger in a loud voice.

70

'He's probably writing about noise in squares or dogs fouling the pavement opposite the Horse Guards' Parade. It's all right, he's deaf.'

'What do you want to talk to me about?' I asked. Swinger looked at me with cold eyes and took a cigar out of his pocket. He didn't offer me one.

'I want to know which side you're on,' he said, lighting the cigar.

'Which side?' I said.

'Yes, which side,' repeated Swinger. 'Perhaps any super-ficial observer of our island ways would come to the conclu-sion that there aren't any sides, that everything flows up-wards and outwards, merges, and is generally transformed by money. But it isn't so, as you are perfectly well aware. There are only the common people on the one hand, and the gentlemen on the other.' He held up his hand. 'Don't pro-test, Mr Carson. Don't talk to me about the arts and sciences. Don't talk to me about state scholarships, or the sons of peers who get into the Top Twenty.'

'I wasn't going to,' I said.

'I repeat,' continued Dr Swinger, 'there are only the com-mon people and the gentlemen. Between these two there is a vast hodge-podge called, loosely, the middle-class. Most of these are trying to be gentlemen, but they always fail. You can't make a silk purse out of a sow's ear. In this hodge-podge you get journalists, actors, TV personalities, shop-keepers and MP's. And, of course, scientists.'

'What about the artists?' I asked.

'You should know all about that,' said Swinger. 'Artists are the slaves of the whole community, baring their miserable souls for the sake of being noticed by other slaves. Some are clever enough or wretched enough or stupid enough to be exploited by business men, and they can even make fortunes, but they are still a national joke.

'The common people, who are now getting used to being flattered, are little different from animals, except that animals are cleaner and make more attractive noises. You can't say you really like those hideous accents. They are eating far too much, earning too much—have you ever watched those television "comics"?—and even thinking too much. . . .'

'Just a moment,' I said, laughing. 'What about the gentlemen?'

'The gentlemen,' said the Doctor, 'are despicable and puerile, but they are what all the others want to be. There is a psychical line, a sort of frontier, beyond which these outsiders cannot really pass. It is possible, at a glance, to distinguish them from the real thing. Massed behind the frontier are the business men and the abstract painters and the philanthropists desperately looking for visas.'

'And what is all this leading to?' I asked.

The doctor puffed away at his cigar. 'Have you told anybody about your theory concerning Jackson and Gold?'

'You are the only one,' I said.

'What about Jonathan Glory?'

'I think he suspects something,' I said, 'and he tried to find out the truth, but I didn't say anything.'

'You haven't said a word to anyone else?' he asked.

'Nobody,' I said.

'That's good,' said the doctor. 'I think you may be on the right side, after all. In any case, I can tell you this. I believe it. I believe what you told me. I believe that Gold's identity changed places with the identity of Jackson. I am aware that there are manifestations of the human psyche which are unknown to, or have been forgotten by modern man. I am also aware that Jackson, today, is going to kill "Bugs" Norton—who, incidentally, is, or was, one of my best clients.'

'And what are you going to do about it?' I asked.

'Absolutely nothing,' said the Doctor, stubbing out his cigar. 'Nothing at all. Nor are you. If either of us made the slightest move, we would both be certified and confined to mental asylums. So would Gold and Jackson. But there is an even more important reason for not trying to disclose anything.'

'What's that?' I asked, rising from my seat.

'The Government would fall,' said Dr Swinger calmly, 'and war might break out.' I started to leave the club lounge, when Swinger came up behind me and took my arm. ' "Bugs" Norton,' he whispered, 'is a very dangerous Communist.'

Nine

I stared at Inspector Gladcliff's glass eye. For some inexplicable reason it looked slightly bloodshot, while the natural one shone with its normal brightness and health. I shifted my gaze to this one, and lit a cigarette. 'I am worried about the Home Office,' said the Inspector. 'There are too many women in Parliament—and half-women too—and they soften the natural virility of the constitution. In other words, someone may talk.' I was slap-up against the blood-shot eye again, and there was a tiny shiver somewhere in my backbone.

'I suppose you are referring to me,' I said.

73

'What makes you say that?' asked Gladcliff in a quiet voice.

'Various people have been getting at me,' I said. I didn't look at the eye. 'As though I was a spy,' I said.

'Who, for instance?' asked Gladcliff.

'Swinger,' I said, 'Doctor Swinger.'

'He's an old woman,' said the Inspector, 'and he's not a doctor. He's in a branch of Military Intelligence. I can't give you the number, because it's unlisted. He's on his own and he's got a free hand. And he's made a bloody mess of things. And we have to back him up, every single member of the Force.' We were sitting in the Way Out Club, drinking coffee, and the one single tree in the street, bang outside the window, was dancing with the music of spring.

When a blackbird sings
I'm you, you're me

'I suppose you wouldn't talk,' said the Inspector casually.

'I wouldn't talk,' I said, 'because I don't know anything to talk about. And if I did know anything to talk about, I wouldn't talk anyway, because I simply haven't got the courage. I'm not built that way. Even when I walk home at night I always look over my shoulder.'

'So do I,' said the Inspector. 'Who else was "at" you?'

'Jonathan Glory,' I said. 'He took me out on one of his jobs and then he tried to pump me about something.'

'About what?' asked the Inspector.

'About . . .' I searched for the right words '. . . about things in Heaven and Earth . . . you know. That bit in Shakespeare.'

'Shakespeare wasn't in the curriculum,' said the Inspector, beaming his glass eye on me. 'It was a good thing you didn't tell him anything,' he said. 'He's another old woman, but he's

74

bloody dangerous. I can tell you this, I wouldn't personally kill anybody, not even on a battlefield. Glory's a stream-lined sadist, if ever there was one. I've heard some pretty stories about him in France during the Occupation.' He seemed to relax suddenly and his face crumpled into the parody of a smile. 'In any case, I'm glad you won't talk.'

We ordered something to drink. 'I see Lady Lingley is here. She's in Jackson's office. I'm always surprised at women being so bloodthirsty. Particularly the beautiful ones. Not like men, in a soddish sort of way, but like cats and spiders. Or sundews. Have you ever seen a sundew?'

'I used to collect them,' I said, 'in Devonshire. On the bogs. Pretty little plants that eat flies.'

'A very minute delicate perfume they have,' said the Inspector.

'Like fairy-land,' I said.

'Now then, come off it,' cried the Inspector shifting back to his glass eye. 'She's the daughter of the Duke of Brancaster,' said Gladcliff, almost smacking his lips. He obviously revelled in titles. 'He's a very rich man indeed, but he was displeased with his daughter, so they say. They've made it up now, though. As far as I'm concerned, what Lady Penelope says goes.' And the same for me, I thought. But I meant it a lot more than the Inspector, and in a different way.

'Another piece of news,' said Gladcliff, who was obviously in the mood for a good gossip. 'That man is around here again.'

'Which man?' I asked.

'The man who came here a few weeks ago and created a disturbance. He put me in a very difficult situation. We've made inquiries and it was either that man or Jackson who killed Lena on Hampstead Heath. You remember Lena?'

'I remember her,' I said. As a matter of fact I had really almost forgotten her, and I suddenly felt a sort of sick, sad feeling, the feeling you have when you say good-bye to girls at enormous railway stations and say you love them, and you cry, and you know you will never see them again and you will utterly forget them. And you are a loving person.

'She was a good girl,' said the Inspector.

'She was a very nice girl,' I said, 'but who is this man?'

'Apparently he's a bank clerk who works in Swiss Cottage, and he appears to have some sort of grudge about something. Perhaps he's mad. He works in a bank and is married. I don't think his wife is exactly happy. That's all we really know about him.'

'That's not much,' I said.

'But he knows everything about us,' said Gladcliff, absolutely everything. And he's been seen hanging about in the street. It adds to the general difficulty, you see. We haven't enough police.'

> The moonlight that I see
> Is the moonlight that you see
> The music and the flowers
> Are ours
> Eternally.

Inspector Gladcliff suddenly leant forward. 'You're a funny sort of fellow,' he said, turning the kindly eye to me. 'I suppose most of you artists are. Heads in the clouds, don't know a fiver from a one-pound note.' He put his hand in the inside pocket of his coat and took out an envelope. 'Perhaps this might help tide you over till the next spot of inspiration.' He handed me the envelope and I promptly opened it. It contained about five hundred pounds in ten-pound notes.

'What's this for?' I asked.

'A really good holiday in the sun,' said Gladcliff. 'Away from it all. You certainly deserve it, sweating away at that typewriter while the rest of us are enjoying ourselves. A cruise, for instance. Duty-free at the bar and pretty girls in bikinis on the sun-deck.' I hesitated, and then pocketed the money. That's the way I am. 'It's a funny business,' said the Inspector, drumming his fingers on the table. 'What people get involved in. It's no good saying you're free or on your own. Maybe you're born free, but I doubt even that. You just go somewhere, minding your own business, and there you are, you're caught in a web. Of course, it can work both ways, good or bad, it depends on your luck.'

'You mean you're caught,' I said.

'You're not kidding,' said the Inspector. 'I'm well and properly hoist. I'd like to be able to tell you something about it, it would clear a bit of the murky air, but I can't take the risk.'

'Could you explain roughly?' I asked.

'Sort of,' said Gladcliff with a laugh. 'Everbody's sitting on a scandal and the further you can get away from the stink of this particular scandal the better. It's an international scandal, a world scandal. It's got to be damped down by anybody and everybody who call themselves patriots or there could be a forest fire.'

'That's a pretty dramatic statement,' I said, feeling the five hundred pounds burning my pocket as well.

'A few heads will roll yet,' said Gladcliff, 'once friend Norton has bitten the dust. I intend to hold on to mine, and I advise you to hold on to yours.' He suddenly gripped my arm and his fingers were like steel. 'I advise you not to ask anybody funny questions about Norton. Just forget the whole thing.

77

One of those typical Soho incidents.' He got up and walked to the door, then stopped and turned towards me. 'Go on that cruise. The bougainvillea is exquisite in Las Palmas this time of the year.'

'Jackson,' I said, 'I think you should try another one of those experiments.'

'Out of the question,' he said, looking at me with that still strange, still unfamiliar horrible face which held nothing of the mild, industrious charm of Gold. 'I have changed course.' Terribly, I knew what he meant.

'I thought you'd be too level-headed for anything like that,' I said. 'For anything so dramatic or romantic.' Then I realised that I'd made a mistake. I wouldn't be supposed to know anything about his state of mind.

'Romantic,' he repeated. 'That's a funny word to use, isn't it?'

'The idea of changing course seems, at this moment, romantic,' I said. 'In the first place you wanted to opt out of the human condition altogether. You made your experiment, something went wrong, you changed into somebody else and you're right in the middle of the nastiest, most dangerous set of circumstances anyone could imagine. Some of them you know, but there are still others which I'm learning about and, believe me, you're in a bloody mess. You've no chance of survival. None at all.'

'I don't care,' said Jackson with a stubborn expression. 'I repeat that I've changed course.'

'You've given up magic,' I said.

'On the contrary,' he said, 'I'm more than ever confirmed in it. There is nothing else of the slightest interest or importance. I have simply decided not to conduct another experiment.'

'What about the birds?' I asked, with a laugh. Jackson looked at me with disgust.

'The birds are free and flying is sweet. That can wait for me. I may as well tell you everything.'

'I've guessed already,' I said. 'It's the young lady now in your office.'

'That's true,' said Jackson slowly.

'You're in love,' I said.

'That would be it,' said Jackson, looking down at the floor.

'People are only something when they are illuminated,' said Jackson. 'People who are not illuminated are merely hulks. The illumination can be in birds or houses or trees— or people.'

'That's nice for the people,' I said sarcastically, although I knew what he meant. 'Humanity has gained a convert.'

'It hasn't,' said Jackson. 'That's where you're wrong. Penelope isn't a person, any more than I am a person. That's how I stand. I leave all the gregarious back-slapping to you. Now you . . .' he pointed at me with the hideous smile I could never really get used to. 'You're the jolly fellow who's really fond of people.' I didn't answer that remark.

'You said Penelope wasn't a person,' I said. 'What did you mean? Did you mean she was a fairy?' Jackson didn't answer at once. Then he smiled again slowly.

'That's what I meant,' he said, 'and that's what I believe. And if you laugh at me for saying that, I can promise you trouble.'

'You're well in the part, aren't you?' I said. 'I've only been trying to warn you. I've been doing my best to get you to disappear before the bomb explodes. And after all, I'm the only

79

person you know who is aware of the real situation. At least I hope so, for your sake. And, as it so happens, I'm the only person you know who also believes in magic.'

'I've changed course,' repeated Jackson in a dull voice.

Charles the barman entered the club and walked over to Jackson and tapped him on the shoulder. 'There's a lady outside wants to speak to you.'

'What sort of a lady?' asked Jackson.

'She's a well set up sort of lady,' said Charles, 'but she's in a proper state. She's been through it, no doubt about that, I wouldn't give her odds-on. She says she's got to see you. It's a matter of life and death, that's the words she used.'

'Pretty strong words,' said Jackson. 'Ask her to come in,' Charles left the club and returned with a woman who had obviously just stopped herself crying. It was Stella Gold. Her face had lost all its colour and she moved with a stoop. Hardly any of her original attractiveness remained. She stared at me without speaking and then sat down like an automaton.

'Anthony, it's good to see you,' she said. 'Everything is in a terrible mess. I don't know what to do.' I held her hand, there was nothing else I could do. I looked at Jackson and saw him staring at her with a mixture of amazement, protectiveness and embarrassment. It was something of a bizarre situation. Stella neither knew who Jackson was, nor whom he had been, and it was hardly possible for him to explain.

'It's my husband,' said Stella. 'He's planning to rob that bank in about a fornight. I've seen his plans, but he doesn't have any idea that I know anything about it. Then he told me last night that he was going to come to the Reservation Club to get in touch with the manager.'

'That's me,' said Jackson.

80

'How do you do,' said Stella.

'My name's "Grey" Jackson,' he said. 'I don't think I know your husband.'

'My husband's name is Richard Gold,' said Stella. 'He works in a bank in Swiss Cottage.'

'This is his wife, Stella,' I said, making the introduction a trifle late owing to the rather difficult circumstances.

'He also said something about a murder,' said Stella. 'He said there was going to be a murder. At about four-thirty, he said. Of course, I think my husband's gone mad. I've known him ten years and it's only in the last few weeks that he's suddenly started behaving like Edward G. Robinson.' She suddenly actually seemed to want to laugh, but instead she burst into tears. Jackson and I waited for the storm to subside. There was nothing either of us could do.

'Listen, Stella,' I said eventually, 'don't you think the best idea is to go home and let things work themselves out. After all, there's nothing you can personally do about it.'

'When Gold arrives here,' said Jackson, 'we'll discuss the matter—whatever it may be—and then he'll go home and tell you all about it.'

'But he won't tell me all about it,' cried Stella. 'He never tells me anything except to get him bottles of whisky and boxes of rotten cigars, and then he knocks me about and breaks all the crockery.'

'Hell,' said Jackson, biting his lip.

'He's absolutely murderous,' said Stella, 'and I can actually sense the vileness of his thoughts vibrating through the clouds of cigar smoke and the stench of alcohol.'

'It might be your imagination,' said Jackson.

'It's nothing to do with my imagination,' cried Stella. 'He talks in his sleep.'

F

81

'I still think you ought to go home right away,' said Jackson. 'We're going to be rather busy here.'

'He's right,' I said. 'You really must go home. Let things settle down.'

'Very well,' said Stella, with tears in her eyes. 'I'll go now.'

She stood up and looked around the room of the club as though she might find something, anything—however small or insignificant—which would reassure her about the meaning of life. Then she ran from the room.

'It's a bit of a mess,' said Jackson, looking down at the floor.

'That's what I told you,' I said.

'That damned bird,' said Jackson.

'I'm surprised you should talk like that,' I said, 'even now.'

'Why?' he asked.

'I should have thought you'd have stuck to your guns,' I said.

'This is no time for metaphysics,' he said, looking at me with an ugly scowl. At that moment a man entered the room. It was Gold. He looked neat, respectable, well-meaning, the sort of man you could imagine always perfectly integrated into the paper world of profit and loss. I could see nothing of the new Gold in him. He stood still for a minute, looking from my face to Jackson's. I felt it was not up to me to make any statement or introduction, but to let the situation develop in its own way. Eventually Gold's eyes settled on Jackson's. I was reminded of the encounter of two ants on some deserted forest highway, antennae probing the hostile, oddly familiar wind, ready for flight or battle. Or two ghosts haunting the same corridor. Then Gold gave a slight smile.

'Mr Jackson, I presume,' he said. Jackson's face slowly returned the smile.

'And you are, no doubt, Mr Gold. Please sit down.'

Gold sat down. 'I think we have a few things to talk about,' he said.

'We could have an interesting discussion,' said Jackson. Possibly he was thinking about his wife, but he didn't know where to begin. 'Don't worry about Mr Carson,' he said. 'He's a very old friend of mine, and I am employing him as my secretary.'

'Very good,' Gold said, taking out a cigar case and offering cigars all round. 'We have obviously got to come to some agreement owing to the rather unconventional circumstances.'

'The circumstances are slightly peculiar,' said Jackson, lighting his cigar.

'If we act sensibly,' said Gold, 'we could get ourselves into a very strong position.'

'You mean that we could pool our knowledge and experience,' said Jackson.

'There's no other course left open to us, is there?' asked Gold, smiling very slightly again.

'I would also like to know how it started,' said Gold.

'I started it,' said Jackson, 'I admit that.'

'That's handsome of you,' said Gold.

'I didn't intend this,' said Jackson. 'You could call it a mistake.' There was quite a long pause.

'There's no good crying over spilt milk,' said Gold. 'We'll have to cut the cackle and get down to work. A rough draft, anyway.'

'I've got business in a few hours,' said Jackson, 'and a certain amount of preparation.'

'I know all about that,' said Gold. 'I was in charge of the original plan. You can count on me to give you any assistance you may need. I shall be in the vicinity.'

'Thank you very much,' said Jackson, 'but I would prefer

to perform on my own. It's a sort of test, if you understand what I mean.'

'I admire initiative,' said Gold. 'I propose to call on you tomorrow. Say around twelve o'clock.' Gold got up from his chair and walked towards the door.

'Just one thing,' cried Jackson, putting down his cigar. 'Go easy on Stella.'

Ten

I was sitting in Jackson's office when Phyllis walked in. She stood beside the desk uncertainly, and I asked her to sit down. I could see she had something on her mind. 'We've hardly talked to each other, have we?' she said. 'I think it's a good thing for people to know artists. It makes them gentler. I mean for people like my husband and so on.'

'That may be true in some cases,' I said.

'Have you always been an artist?' she asked.

'Quite a lot of people would say not,' I said.

'I'm really very lonely,' said Phyllis, folding her hands and then putting them to the bulge of her neck. She was dressed in a sort of charcoal grey which didn't suit her. 'I don't mean that I don't see many people,' she said, 'but they're really very harmless people, aren't they.'

'Very distinguished,' I said.

'It's not that,' said Phyllis. 'Some of them are really quite

84

distinguished, I grant you that, but not one of them would say "boo" to a goose. Shall I tell you why?'

'Please do,' I said.

'It's because my husband always wanted it that way. Ever since we were married. He was very jealous. He still is, even though he hardly ever speaks to me. I was always made to have dull friends. I wasn't allowed to even speak to anyone I really liked. And all that business about my singing.'

'But you have a lovely voice,' I said. 'I've heard you singing upstairs.'

'I always hated singing,' she said. 'You could say my husband invented it.'

'I was a terrible flirt when I was a girl,' said Phyllis. 'Oh, I was such a flirt. I can still feel inside me a sort of gay feeling. A lovely falling feeling. Do you know what I mean?' She suddenly huddled in her chair and folded her hands again in her lap. 'But it wasn't that I wanted to talk about,' she said. 'There was—there is—a man I've managed to know. Do you know who he is?'

'I think I do,' I said. 'It's Norton.'

'Norton,' said Phyllis. 'I'm talking to you like this because I trust you. I don't know why I trust you, but I do. I very much want you to help me. I think my husband is an enemy of Norton. Because of me, and because of something else. Something they did together—I don't know anything about it—but I'm terribly afraid. I have a feeling something is going to happen to Norton.'

Phyllis clutched my hand. 'It's happened to other people before, but I didn't care about them. They were all dull and beastly. Do you know, Norton has never forgotten my birthday?'

'What can I do?' I asked.

'Try and warn him,' said Phyllis in a whisper. 'Try and tell him to try and get away. Ask him to tell you where he will be. Because I will go and join him.'

She gripped my hand harder. 'Do that for me,' she cried.

Eleven

WE were sitting in Jackson's office in a neatly placed row of chairs, as though for a theatrical performance. There was Penelope, Glory and myself. Glory looked at his watch in a very efficient manner and checked it with a clock on Jackson's desk. 'Nine minutes more,' he said, 'and then the balloon will go up.'

'Why are the English so calm and efficient about gambling and violence?' asked Penelope.

'Because they are not bored then,' said Glory. 'The English only get more or less hysterical when they deal with abstractions.' He turned towards me. 'Have you ever spent a considerable time in a very large retrospective exhibition of abstract paintings?'

'I've passed through one or two of them fairly quickly,' I said.

'I once spent a whole hour studying eighty-six of them,' said Glory. 'I was determined to get to the bottom of the problem. Once I was outside the gallery I stood on the pavement shouting. Actually shouting. Of course, I was arrested but later released on bail.'

'You're not supposed to think about them,' I said. 'That's the whole point.' I didn't believe the story anyway. I had seen at least two abstracts in his house at Regent's Park, and very good ones they were too.

I looked at Penelope who was now in the open, but I didn't look too carefully at her in case she should scuttle back among the bracken. I was in a meadow of love, in that perfect young summer weather which is awaiting everybody. I felt clear and powerful, but I was trembling and hope was opening and shutting like flowers. Years ago it had happened but the weather didn't hold and the grass faded. It was my fault. You think it will always be there and you can laugh or complain as you like. Then it is dark. On and on you go, and sometimes you see the summer glory in faces or fields, but it is quickly gone. How many years was it? Ten, twenty, a hundred? And here it was once more and the careless armour of my youth had vanished. But, in some absurd way, it seemed as though it hadn't and that Time had slipped back. After the third glance she looked back at me and left her eyes on me for a time. Perhaps we both knew something, and I held this something close to me, whatever it could be.

'I hope everything goes to plan,' said Glory, showing his teeth. 'And I'm not merely being bloodthirsty. If the affair didn't go right it could end up in a pretty untidy mess for a lot of people.'

'I suppose it depends which side you're on,' I said.

Glory looked at me very heard for a moment or two. 'That's true,' he said. 'The only people who are worth while have made up their minds about that. Friends or enemies.'

'It's true,' said Penelope in a low voice. 'It's a thing you can't pretend about. You can't be in both places.'

'Single-mindedness,' cried Glory in a suddenly loud bombastic voice. 'Everything's single-mindedness. I remember during the war. . . .'

'It's going to be one of his stories,' said Penelope.

'I remember,' said Glory, 'I was in a wood with another man. He was one of my Corporals. He was the best of my Corporals. His name was Fred. We were in France, somewhere near Lyons, and we were waiting for a convoy. It wasn't the first time. The bloody Huns had wandered through there two or three times and Fred had always been ready for them. One day we got cut off from all our equipment and all we had was a mess-tin and an iron file. The wonderful things the Corporal did with that mess-tin. He made the rim as sharp as a razor and got stuck behind a blackberry bush and waited for over two hours. He didn't mope one bit, Fred didn't. And when he finally got to work he was nothing short of a master craftsman. He's a butcher now in Leeds, four kids, and helps with the Sunday School. I did a story about him a few months ago for *Woman's Dream*.'

'I read it,' I said. 'Do you really like him that much? It seems impossible.'

'As a matter of fact I didn't like him at all. To tell you the truth, I'm extremely squeamish but I think the War image was splendid, and it's what we need more of now.'

'It would be too noisy,' said Penelope.

The crowds who had been passing directly under the window had suddenly dwindled and the street was now empty. 'The police are sending them around the other way,' said Glory. Gladcliff's an efficient chap. He'll have invented something about a fire or a hold-up.' I could feel tension now. The

88

air was flat, like left soda-water, and it was difficult to breathe. There could have been a thunderstorm coming up or an earthquake or a tidal wave. All three of us moved our chairs closer to the window and waited. 'It's time,' cried Glory. 'Exactly.' At that moment 'Bugs' Norton came into view. He was walking slowly along the pavement and then paused and looked into the window of a tobacconist's shop. I could see his profile, something like a tamed hawk that had been in captivity too long. He took out a cigarette and lit it and then examined the street behind and in front of him.

'Why is he here exactly on time?' I asked. 'He's not under contract.'

'It's legal,' said Glory. 'Norton couldn't be murdered in cold blood.'

'But it is murder,' I said.

'Call it what you like,' said Glory, 'it's legal. That's all that matters. If he was killed privately there would not only be trouble with the Law but with the gangs as well. This place would be burnt to the ground and there'd be mayhem high and low. And I mean "high".'

'But does Norton understand exactly what's happening? Does he know why he's supposed to be here? And has he come by any agreement?'

'It's a duel,' said Glory. 'Just the simple matter of a duel. It's going on all the time. It goes on in Big Business, in the academic world, in Sport, in Love, in children's playgrounds. Everybody's destroying everybody else, mostly with smiles and printed forms and telephone calls. Torture covered over by rhetoric and good manners. Timid people wisely keep away and keep to their sober little crafts. What's going on now is the true basis of society, Primitive Law.' He showed his teeth in a joyless grin and edged closer to the window.

I was watching Norton. He was standing very still beside the tobacconist's shop and I saw his hand drop to his pocket. His arm seemed to twitch half a second before the sound of the explosion, but that was a trick of the brain. He turned his head quickly around and ran towards a ladder which was leaning against the wall beside the shop. He clambered up it and when he had reached the top his left arm was struggling to reach into the pocket on the opposite side of his body. There was the sound of another shot and Norton swayed on the ladder for quite a long time. There was complete stillness, the town could have been dead, carpeted with ashes. Then he fell. It was like watching a man who hadn't learned how to dive properly. Beside me, Penelope cried out like a trapped animal and the sound sank to a moan and then stopped. Norton was spreadeagled on the railings below and something was happening directly under him.

A man ran up the street towards Norton. He started to shout, and for a moment he turned his face up towards the window. It was Jackson. I had never seen the eyes of a man so enormous or so empty of hope and meaning. 'Help,' he shouted, 'help!' and threw himself at the body of Norton, tugging and pulling at it and shouting. There was the sound of another explosion and Jackson fell. He made no sound at all now, but he was trying to get up. But we didn't look long at Jackson. Blood was pouring out of the figure on the railings, and not only blood; there was a tangle of coils, of pipes. I had seen this in the bullring and I desperately defended my mind by trying to remember where it had been. Valencia? Valladolid? Glory got up and slowly left the room. I could hear the door close gently. Penelope stayed where she was. I had to turn and look at her. Her face was a peculiar shade of white, it had a touch of green. It didn't make her look beautiful or ugly, it removed her from life into something close to eternal death. Into a place you don't want to enter.

Some people were now walking along the street. There was a middle-aged man and a woman. The woman was carrying a shopping bag. They looked calm. Then there was a young man, the sort who could have been on the fringe of a pop group. They passed Jackson and the figure on the railings without even looking at them. Then a car drove down the street and I could hear people laughing. A dog barked. It was going to rain.

'That's what they like,' said Penelope in a low voice. 'That's what they like.' She took hold of my hand and it was very cold, like an icy river.

'I was married to Norton,' she said. I jumped up. I had been in a spell. I was afraid. I was afraid for everybody but mostly for myself. I ran out of the room and down the stairs and out on to the street.

But I was not the first one to get there. There was a woman crouched over the body of Norton and when she turned her head I could see her mouth opening and shutting like the mouth of a fish in poisoned water. But no sound came from it. It was Phyllis. Then, suddenly, as though a sound-track had been repaired, the screams emerged and she fell on the quivering body, but as she fell there was a third explosion. Jackson's wife threw out her arms and her last terrible song was still for ever.

PART TWO

One

THE dusty fly-by-night room was marigold bright in the morning. The sun had pushed through the hideous, heavy curtains and striped the floor with summer. We were in a hotel in Shaftesbury Avenue. It was a railway station of a hotel for commercial travellers, trapped lovers, lonely soldiers posted for death, old people waiting for news. It was the ugliest, most beautiful hotel in London.

'I'll ring for breakfast,' I said. 'The breakfasts here are marvellous and you get Oxford marmalade.'

'I see you know the hotel,' said Penelope.

'Yes,' I said, 'during the war. I was always saying goodbye to a girl, but I never left the country. That was the girl I told you I loved.'

'I suppose it was because you were a coward,' said Penelope. I turned and looked at the window.

'Not that I mind,' she said, and kissed me. 'I wish it had been then,' she said. She meant I should have been slim and more or less at the beginning. She suddenly threw the clothes off the bed and was naked. I was back in the woodland, the leaves were over my head. She was the Queen and the creature. . . .

CENSORED

There was a knock on the door and a very plain, old-fashioned maid entered the room with the breakfast and newspapers. There was no doubt that she had been delivering breakfasts since the coronation of Edward the Seventh and had made a fortune in guilty tips. I gave her ten shillings to keep the happiness in the room. Then we opened the newspapers and in the middle page of the *Daily Glass* was an article by Jonathan Glory. It was entitled CRIME AND THE FAMILY:

'In the heart of the Family (wrote Glory) there is harmony and understanding and a mutual respect for the values and decencies which have made the majority of British people what they are. In the heart of the British family there may be the occasional anxieties and doubts which assail us all. But the clouds disappear and the British sun soon comes shining through. Without this shared knowledge of inherited respect fer decencies and the Christian way of life, what are we? Mere pitiable dross, to be tempted by any and every whim of idleness or lust or blasphemy, floundering in the quicksands of immorality and being swallowed up.

'I was thinking about these things (continued Glory) when my feet chanced to take me towards Soho, haunts of flashy Continental restaurants and sleazy strip-tease joints. Almost immediately after entering the area, I became aware of something painful which almost caught at my throat. I am, as you know, a man who soldiered right through the war and who underwent many painful and tragic experiences—inseparable, alas, from such activities, however just and right in their enterprise but I had never before encountered such a depth of despair. It was a feeling of suddenly being cut off. Cut off from the normal main-springs of happiness, of children's laughter, of friend greeting friend. Cut off, in short, from the family.

'And I was right in my impression. Here indeed were the forces of Evil, all around me. I turned the corner of a street and heard a pistol shot. I saw a man fall. I watched him climb a ladder. There was another shot and this wretched man (can I say motherless man) fell off the ladder and was impaled on some railings below him. I stood there, a Witness, a Bystander of folly and evil. Later a woman ran out of a house, possibly to protect this man. There was another shot, and the poor woman (with her little gleam of humanity) also fell to the ground. And what was the sequel to all this misery and horror I can tell you. I can tell you, and I'm not ashamed to tell you, that even as I write now, there are actual tears in my eyes. Not a single person who passed by paid the slightest attention to these wretched, condemned prisoners of the lost lands of Soho. Here, in London, in this teeming area, any sign of the Good Samaritan had been wiped off the face of the earth.

'At last I found a policeman, and it was like returning home to one's loved-ones to see his healthy ruddy face. I recounted to him what had occurred and he shook his head and said slowly: "There is no God here." "*There is no God here*". Those were his words, and they are engraved on my heart. Let them be engraved on yours. . . .'

'Beautiful,' said Penelope gravely while she ate some of the thick marmalade off a spoon, 'and he probably shot those people himself. No, not really. But he could, I think, if he wasn't so ambitious.'

'Do you mind that?' I asked her.

'No. Not a bit really,' she said. 'I don't think I mind about people being killed as long as it's not children.'

'Why did you marry Norton?'

'Because it was very romantic, and at that time he seemed very good-looking. He was better looking than the man I was supposed to marry, for instance. At least I thought so at the time. And I wanted to get away from the Life. It was hanging over me.'

'What sort of Life?' I asked.

'The Good, Wonderful, Sheltered Life. Like a porcelain bowl. Those Right sort of faces that have been through the wrong things properly. Lying in sheets like clouds. Bored with peacocks and quaint gardeners. Bach and the M.F.H.'

'Sounds lovely,' I said. 'I've never been near it.'

'That life was always open to me. It still is. I was divorced from Norton after terrible rows. I went back to my family in Devonshire and loved it quite quickly—I become happy very easily—and my intended husband forgave me. They always do.'

Penelope started to dress. I knelt down and put on her shoes. She stopped dressing. 'The other Life pulls at me even more strongly. The stark, dirty one with bright colours. Like the slums of Naples. I've always wanted to be absolutely lost there and stripped of everything.'

'And then saved from it,' I said. Penelope laughed.

'Oh, not necessarily,' she said. 'I'm fairly brave.'

'I think so,' I said, trembling with love.

'And now there's a third Life,' she said, 'with Jackson.'

'With Jackson,' I cried. I felt sick. In a very small moment that seemed a long time I had crawled to a door that I could no longer open. It was locked.

'Yes,' she said, laughing, and then stroked my hair. 'I'm sorry,' she said. 'I am sorry.'

'Damn you for being beautiful,' I said, but so softly she couldn't have heard it.

'You won't laugh at me if I tell you something, will you?'

'No,' I said.

'It's something I thought I would never say in all my life. I am going to become an albatross.' She leant over me with eyes that were suddenly blazing with the green of diamonds and then she threw herself back on the bed laughing helplessly.

We were both dressed, seated on the bed, and the sun had moved away from the window. It was cooler. 'I know all about the whole thing,' said Penelope. At first I didn't understand what she meant, and then the truth broke in.

'You understand about what happened to Jackson?' I said.

'Everything,' she said, 'he told me everything. About how he was a man called Gold and how he tried to turn himself into an albatross and how the experiment went wrong and he turned into Jackson. And Jackson turned into Gold.'

'I'm amazed,' I said.

'What are you amazed at?' asked Penelope.

'That he should have told you,' I said. But, to tell the truth, I wasn't. It seemed perfectly right and obvious.

'And do you really and honestly believe it?' I asked.

'Of course,' said Penelope. 'I don't see why I shouldn't believe it. I find it difficult to believe in the radio or the electric light, but I don't find it difficult to believe in this.' There was quite a long pause.

'And you really are going away with him?' I asked in what I knew was rather a foolish voice.

'Very far away,' said Penelope, and we both started laughing.

'But he's a hideous man,' I said, 'and you've told me how you only like romantic, noble-looking men.'

'You're not romantic or noble-looking,' she said in a hard voice. This tone made me feel very miserable. 'But you see,' she said, holding my hand with the early morning softness, 'you showed me that early photograph of yourself and I made that into you. That's what I did with Jackson. He showed me a photograph of himself taken when he was Gold. Gold's face was quite fine and beautiful and I have managed to put that into Jackson's unfortunate face. I really love him.' This made me still angrier.

'How can you love a multiple murderer?' I asked.

'He told me about that too,' said Penelope. 'It wasn't Jackson who shot Norton or Phyllis. It was somebody else.'

'Who?' I asked, as if I didn't really know who it was.

'That doesn't matter,' said Penelope. 'All that matters is that it wasn't Jackson.'

'But what is it about Jackson that makes you want to try and do this preposterous thing?' I asked. 'You're not a licensed magician yourself, are you?'

'I've never thought about those sort of things,' she said.

'Well, what are you thinking about?'

'Happiness,' said Penelope.

'You can't think about that all the time,' I said 'In fact you can't really think about happiness at all.'

'You can prepare for it,' said Penelope. 'Something like

100

dancing.' She bent forward, her hair fell down and she was back in the woodland. She looked up again. 'I can't talk about it,' she said. 'It's what I've chosen. I could have chosen the others.' We were silent for a very long time. There was a knock on the door and the archaic maid peeped in.

'Will you be staying tonight?' she asked.

'No,' I almost shouted.

'There's another thing,' I said. 'I want to try to get to the bottom of it. After all, when all is said and done, I am a friend of Jackson.'

'I'm glad,' said Penelope. 'Oh, I'm that all right. And I suppose you know they're going to try and kill him.'

'Yes, I know that,' she said, 'and I know why. At least I know part of it.'

'Can you explain?' I asked.

'It's called the United Nations affair,' said Penelope. 'Not openly, of course, but I've heard it mentioned now and then. Somebody disappeared or was done away with. He was supposed to be a very important man. I don't know much about the details, but they were all involved in it, Jackson, Glory, Norton and a few others. There was a man called Swinger, I think, whom I met once and found very boring. Whatever actually happened, they're terribly keen that nobody else finds out about it.'

'Who are meant by nobody else?' I asked.

'People outside their group, I suppose. I don't know how big that group is. It may be enormous. I don't really know anything about it, except that Jackson was trying to compromise this United Nations man and took a photograph of him doing something or other discreditable in the Reservation. But there is one thing I can tell you. There is one person who can give you some information.'

'Who?' I asked.

'Charles, the barman in the Way Out. But he wouldn't say anything unless you mentioned my name and told him I had asked him to help you.'

'I'll try him,' I said.

I was lucky to find Charles alone in the Way Out. I told him what Penelope had said. 'Well,' said Charles, pouring me a drink, 'I'd rather not talk about it. The whole thing's bloody dynamite and I want to try and stay alive. But if Lady Lingley wants me to tell you anything I will, and bugger the consequences. The United Nations man was a fellow called Marietti. He was a little darkish sort of a man with those sort of thick horn-rimmed glasses you see on the Telly in those interviews. He came here five or six times. It was about five years ago. I remember two or three times he came here with a funny looking dog. It had an odd sort of name and I remember laughing about it. Let me think.' Charles leant on the bar with his head on his hand, then looked me straight in the eye. 'I've got it now,' he said. 'It's name was Gruffy. Bloody funny name, and he never made a sound.'

'But what happened?' I asked. 'Never mind about the dog.'

'Apparently,' said Charles, 'this fellow Marietti was a very important member of the United Nations Organisation and he was stopping over in London to confer with the Government. Then he was going on to New York. He had some sort of plan or other. I heard it mentioned somewhere that this plan had been more or less accepted by all of what they call the Major Powers. Something to do with disarmament, world starvation, birth control. The lot. He wasn't popular in these quarters, I can tell you.'

'And then?' I almost shouted.

102

'And then,' said Charles, 'and mind you I'm not too sure of my facts. . . .'

'Never mind,' I cried, 'whatever you think happened.'

'Well, he was lured over here, I think, and they gave him champagne and they introduced him to that girl Lena. Do you remember her? She got bumped off.'

'Yes, I remember her,' I said.

'Go on.'

'Mr Jackson—or maybe it was Mr Glory—took a photograph of them together—it must have been a pretty remarkable photograph.'

'Never mind about the photograph,' I cried. 'What happened after that?' Charles's face went suddenly blank. Whether he was scared or whether he really didn't know any more I was unable to discover. I repeated my question.

'I don't know what happened,' he said. 'Not a bloody thing. All I *did* hear were a couple of pistol shots up above the club. Or there may have been three.' He scratched his head. 'But there weren't more than three,' he said.

'Is there anything else you can remember at all? Any sort of detail?' Charles thought for some time, looking up at the ceiling.

'Yes, of course,' he said suddenly. 'It's all in some papers. In some sort of documents. I know where they are. They're in a secret drawer in Mr Jackson's office.' His eyes left mine and he seemed to be regretting what he had said to me.

'How do you know that?' I asked, leaning over the bar counter.

'I'll tell you the truth, sir,' said Charles. 'I was listening at the keyhole.'

I had to laugh. I took out my wallet and gave him quite a fair bit of Jackson's money.

Two

COULD see Jackson was frightened. I didn't feel very good myself. As we both walked together through the urbane wilderness of Kensington Gardens it was obvious to see his limp. 'It isn't serious,' he said. 'Just a flesh wound.' We sat down beside the Serpentine. Small groups of people, in love, without money, bored or half-smothered by dogs and children idled by the shores of the false lake. We sat down in a couple of vacated deck-chairs. 'I've found the documents,' said Jackson. 'What Charles told you was right. But it's even bigger in scope than that. It involves five other countries, naturally including America. I had no idea the Reservation was so widely and thoroughly organised. You'd be surprised at the names of some of the Founder members. I've got the list here. I thought you might like to look at it. There are two Prime Ministers and that Washing Machine man and the Union organiser. And there's nothing to choose between. . . .

CENSORED

'. . . My God,' I said.
'I'm burning it right away,' said Jackson, and he lit a match and set fire to the piece of paper. 'They talk about the Mafia,' he said. 'You're not supposed to take people seriously who eat

garlic. But this lot are worse than the Mafia. They're the respectable ones. They're the so-called Gentlemen. They're air-conditioned monsters, a universal brotherhood who bludgeon you to death by monopolies, with a façade of beauty queens and drip-dry television announcers. They condemn the world to perpetual war and starvation.

'That's why this gang got rid of Marietti. He was working on a disarmament plan which was on the point of being accepted. There was something about contraception too. There was a reference to trying to curb the Royal Family. That is the last thing they want, the very last thing, they can't exist without war or over-population or the menace of war and famine. War means money. And perhaps there isn't anything but the Golden Kiss.

'From the documents, I can't quite make out who actually shot Marietti, or whether he's even dead. It was either Gold or Norton. But certainly you can see who was one of the heads of the Organisation, and that is Jonathan Glory. Inspector Gladcliff either joined the Reservation voluntarily or was compromised, and there must have been, must still be a fair number of the Police Force on their payroll. Gold has a criminal record as long as your arm.

'I'm not going to be mixed up in this. I'm not a martyr or a politician. I'm ashamed to say I live on a purely personal basis. I admit I got tangled with the idea of possessing and making a lot of money, but I never asked to be turned into a gangster. Certainly, if I had the slightest thread of social responsibility I would do something about this and expose the whole bloody crew of the bastards. I wouldn't hesitate to risk my neck. I suppose the same thing goes for you.'

'I don't want to be mixed up in it,' I said. 'I feel the same as you about it.' Jackson laughed.

'I suppose you bring up the old excuse that you're an artist, a sort of uncommitted recorder of the times.'

'Possibly,' I said, 'or possibly neither of us has the courage.' We watched a duck edging itself slowly on to the bosom of the water.

'I think I've been fairly consistent,' said Jackson. 'I've set my mind on a goal. I've aimed at what is almost the unattainable essence of being, a simple yet complicated thing.

'Then I fell in love,' said Jackson.

'You were in love with Stella,' I said.

'All the stars were not in the sky,' said Jackson. 'This present love is day, night, the sky and the sea. It is my only reason for having lived, or living now.' He gave a short laugh and looked embarrassed. 'Besides, everything else apart, Stella wouldn't know me now. Or ever.'

'I suppose not,' I said.

'So I'm leaving. I'm leaving with Penelope.'

'So I heard,' I said. 'Penelope told me. I suppose you know that I'm in love with Penelope too.'

'Penelope informed me about that,' said Jackson.

'You're not the only one with these transcendental ideas,' I said, and looked away angrily up the other end of the lake. There was a long silence only broken by the duck that had just entered the water and who was suddenly complaining. 'I understand,' I said, 'that you are both leaving by albatross.'

'There's no need to be facetious,' said Jackson. 'That's what we intend to do as quickly as possible. In fact there's nothing else we can do. They'll have another pot-shot at me the next time I show my face in the Reservation.'

'How can you be sure of that?' I asked. 'The last time may only have been a mistake.' Jackson struck me hard on the knee.

106

'You know why as well as I do,' he said. 'The whole gang know everything about the Transformation.' I didn't say anything, but I knew it must be true.

'Therefore,' said Jackson, 'I want you to help me. It is terribly urgent. I certainly don't ask you to help me on account of Penelope, I quite understand that you wouldn't consider that, I wouldn't ask you myself under similar circumstances. I ask your help for the simple reason that I don't want to be killed and I really think you are my friend. That is so, isn't it?'

'Yes,' I said, 'I suppose that's true. What do you want me to do?'

'I want you to go to Stella's house—naturally when Gold's out—and find my albatross formula. It's the only one I possess and I'm pretty sure I can't manage the Transformation without it. As it is, I'm worried about this limp. I don't want to carry it over on to the bird. Will you do it?'

'All right,' I said, 'if you must have it.'

'Will you do it right away? I'll be in my office for the last time this evening.'

We both got up, and for some reason or other shook hands.

'And if you can,' said Jackson, 'bring me some of that special straw. You'll find it up in the attic.'

'It's unspeakable,' said Stella. 'Richard's stacked the whole bathroom full of dynamite.' She looked at me in a dull sort of way, and apart from her radiating an even greater degree of unhappiness, I got the impression that she was suffering from some further ill. It wasn't, in fact, difficult to guess at. She had been drinking. On the centre table in the living-room I could see a half empty bottle of sherry, which certainly wasn't the kind of tipple enjoyed by a man like Gold. 'At first I thought he'd really gone mad,' she said, 'but I've gradually come to consider it as some entirely new pattern he has evolved. But it's not only him alone. It's his friends.'

'What friends?' I asked.

'They come here from time to time. They're quite well-spoken, mind you, and one of them even appears to be a clergyman. They say some extraordinary things. The last time they were here I happened to be in the bathroom—that was before the dynamite was stacked in there—and I could hear some of what they were saying. The bathroom, you see, has a very thin wall and is next to this living-room.'

'What were they talking about?' I asked.

'It was mainly about killing a man called Jackson,' said Stella, 'and there was something about getting rid of somebody called Lady Lingley. My dear husband said the whole thing could be left to him. He said it perfectly calmly. Of course, in my better moments I realise the whole thing's a joke. Men do that sort of thing and you're supposed to laugh. Personally I don't laugh.' Instead, she burst into tears. I sat there looking at her.

'Have a drink,' she said in a damp, strangled voice.

'Thanks,' I said. I poured out a glass of sherry and then I thought I'd pour out another glass for her. She picked up the glass and swallowed all the sherry at one gulp. I kept on looking at her. I was in a conflict of emotions. Why should I feel like this?

Her sobbing ceased, and she began to dry her eyes with a handkerchief. Crying actually suited her. Her eyes shone with sherry and dismay. 'It's such a puzzling life now,' she said, 'but the worst thing is the terrible untidiness. I'm not a hausfrau or anything like that, but this sort of untidiness is simply not fair. It's like trying to empty the sea with a tea-spoon. Don't you remember how neat Richard used to be? Do you think it's anything to do with the satellites? Let's have some more sherry and then I won't cry any more. We might even laugh.' She smiled at me and I poured out some more sherry.

She was really pretty, now, in a desperate way. I had never thought of an affair with her, quite apart from the question of her husband, even though she was slender and attractive and quick. But at this moment she suddenly filled me with a vast attraction. It may have been because of her hunger and the sea and the tea-spoon or some conjunction of planets. I have had my share of love affairs, though I'm not a professional seducer. Some of them have been somewhat discreditable, but the majority not. Like most people—who hardly ever admit it—I have not always risen to the occasion, but with a good wind or, better still, a gale, I have given a good account of myself. I crossed the room and sat beside Stella. After all, she had told me Gold was away for the day.

'What now?' she asked, finishing her sherry. 'Now listen, Stella,' I said, taking her hand. She didn't withdraw it. . . .

'I still feel very untidy,' said Stella, laughing. I got up and dressed, looking down at her. There she was, in a corner of my mind and the shutter went down. Now I had to get Jackson's formula.

'I'll be back in a minute,' I said. I rushed out of the room and entered the living-room where Jackson had his desk. I went to the left-hand side of the desk, as he had told me, and slid back a sort of bolt. Then I went to the back of the desk. A drawer opened, as he had said it would. It was empty. I hunted around the edge of the desk but couldn't find any other bolts. I gave it up. There was nothing else to be done. I went back to Stella's bedroom. The electricity trembled and then shot up like a neon light.

Five minutes later there was a knock on the door. At first it was a fairly quiet knock, but the noise went on, louder and louder. 'Oh, my God,' said Stella. 'It's Richard. I locked the door. This is the end of it.'

'Wait a bit,' I said.

Then the knocking got frantic, and a voice shouted out, 'Open up in the name of the Law.'

'It's the Police,' I said.

'Go out, then,' cried Stella. 'I'll try and dress. Keep them waiting.' I somehow got myself together, tied myself a slovenly tie, went to the door and opened it. The man at the door was Jonathan Glory.

'Just as I thought,' cried Glory, baring his teeth and grinning without joy. 'I'm looking for Jackson. Where is he?'

'He's not here,' I said. 'Why should he be here?'

'Why are you here?' he asked.

'That's my business,' I said.

'It might be your business to die,' said Glory. 'Intelligent people should never try to pick up information they don't really need.' Suddenly he flung himself on top of me, and he was a very strong and heavy man. We floundered about the hall, and I soon knew that he was stronger than me. In a sort of puerile way I shouted at him. 'Marietti,' I cried, 'Marietti.' It was a stupid thing to say, but I couldn't think of anything else. It was directed at his prose style. It was directed at his teeth.

'Very well,' said Glory in a calm voice. 'Very well. From now on you haven't got a pig's chance in hell.' I edged cautiously around him, and I had already decided to give him a rugby tackle—the only decent trick I had ever learnt from my English school days—when he brought out a gun. 'Goodbye,' he said, 'and watch out. This is merely a warning. I'm not the one to finish you off. You know who that'll be.' He shut the door in my face.

Three

IT took me quite a time before I came to the conclusion that I was being followed. It wasn't that anything of a particular nature occurred, it took the form of a nervous, shivery feeling at the back of my head. At the same moment no object, no matter of what kind, that I noticed in the street seemed harmless, not even the curtains moving behind the windows or a cat running down an area steps. I was making for the Leicester Square Underground when I saw a man in a bowler hat standing outside a shop-window. He was definitely staring at me. Also I was certain that I had seen the man before, if not twice before, on the same day. I tried to remember where. He was a thin man

111

in a rather shabby black suit and wore gold-rimmed spectacles. But I told myself this must all be imagination. I stopped beside a newspaper seller and bought an *Evening Standard*, then hurried down the Tube stairs.

I went to the telephone kiosks, struggled with pennies and half-crowns and rang up the Reservation. I got through to Jackson and told him what I had heard from Stella about Gold's plan to kill him and Penelope. 'That's all right,' said Jackson, 'I'll deal with him at once. Don't ring me here again. I'm leaving for good. In case we don't meet again, you'll know where I am.' This last remark seemed a bit flippant, but the tone of his voice was as cold as a cave. I replaced the receiver and got on to the escalator. After I had boarded the train I looked around the compartment and there was the man in the bowler hat, seated up at the far end, smoking a pipe. He was not looking in my direction, obviously with care not to attract my attention. Again I stated to myself that the whole thing was imagination. But I got out of the train at the next station and moved down the platform to board the next one.

Just before the train pulled up, I felt a shove in the back and felt myself stumbling towards the track. I fell on to one hand, turning my head, and saw a man running in the opposite direction. I could see his bowler hat. 'That man,' I shouted at the top of my voice, and someone helped me up. I could see a mass of eyes looking at me as though I had shouted something obscene, and I started running up towards the other end of the platform. I was banging into people and a very large man carrying a suitcase swore at me in a loud voice. 'Bloody foreigner,' he shouted. There wasn't a sign of Bowler Hat, and I got on to the next train and left it four stations later. I ran up the escalators until I could hardly breathe and staggered out on to the street. I signalled wildly for a taxi and while I was waving I was waving for Life and the prolonging of Life and the room in the shady hotel with the archaic maid bringing in the breakfast.

Three minutes later the car went for me. I had only noticed it vaguely at first, it had seemed to be moving quite slowly and then it accelerated with an enormous burst of speed, and I only just managed to jump out of the way. I hadn't time to see anybody properly in the car, except a man wearing dark glasses. By now I was standing behind a lamp-post and the car backed in a few seconds and shot forward into the traffic. A taxi drew up.

'God Almighty,' shouted the driver. 'Seen a ghost?'

'Something like that,' I said.

'You're as white as a sheet,' said the driver.

'I nearly got run over,' I said.

'Some of them bastards shouldn't be allowed on the roads,' said the driver. 'If I had my way I'd put the buggers in detention camps.' I got into the taxi, and automatically gave the driver Dr Swinger's address. In some odd way his name seemed to spell safety. When I looked out of the window I saw the man in the bowler hat standing on the opposite side of the street. He was calmly cleaning his spectacles. Slowly he lifted his eyes and looked at me, replaced his spectacles and took out a revolver. I pulled down the window and shouted. I kept on shouting. The man in the bowler hat quietly replaced the revolver in his pocket, strolled away and then began running through the crowd of pedestrians. He ran like a hare. The taxi-driver opened the door of the taxi and got hold of my arm.

'Are you took bad?' he asked.

'I think it's appendicitis,' I said. 'I'm sorry to give you trouble like this. Drive to that address as quickly as you can.'

H

'I'm afraid there's nothing I can do,' said Dr Swinger, rubbing the red beak of his nose and leaning forward over his desk. 'I would suggest that this whole persecution story of yours, though certainly not consciously fabricated, springs from pure, or impure imagination. If I had the time I would be very glad to examine your particular case. There seems to be some strong possibility of an Oedipus complex with boundless variations.'

'Don't be ridiculous,' I shouted. 'It was you who first told me about the Scandal. Don't you remember?'

'I don't remember telling you anything about a scandal,' said the doctor in a voice that was obviously intended to be calming. 'That is another thing you have unintentionally invented. You are trying to impress me. These sort of cases always do.'

'You don't remember telling me anything about it?' I cried. 'Do you deny you are one of the chiefs of Military Intelligence?' Swinger roared with laughter. It was a good joke.

'This gets better and better,' he cried and stopped laughing. 'Or worse and worse,' he said.

'Haven't you ever heard of Marietti?' I shouted, standing up.

'Never heard of him in my life,' said the doctor. 'What is he, exactly? An abstract painter?' I sat down again.

'If you don't believe me,' I said, 'I certainly don't believe you.'

'Then we're quits,' said Swinger. 'The whole of life is made up of contending opposites.'

I suddenly had an idea. 'Will you give me the address of the Reverend Roger Rout?' I asked.

'With pleasure,' said the doctor. 'You will find him this evening at his Mission Hall next to St Matthew's Church in

Cripplegate. Go there at about six. But I shouldn't talk to him about this, if I were you.'

St Matthew's Mission Hall turned out to be a building like an Army Nissen hut and the surroundings were equally neat and impersonal. From within I could hear the sound of juke-box music and the clatter of fruit-machines. While I was standing in the road near the pavement with my eyes on the hall, I heard the roar of an engine and instinctively ducked on to the pavement. A motor-cycle hurtled by and hammered into the distance. It had missed me by two inches. I was trembling and leant against the fence outside the hall trying not to be sick. A minute or two later I heard the sound of another motor-cycle and a scarlet machine drew up a few feet away. The driver was encased in black leather with a red helmet and his face was almost entirely covered by huge black goggles. He dismounted from the bicycle and moved towards the gate. His goggles turned in my direction and he seemed on the point of stopping, but he went on walking and entered the hut.

After a few more minutes I decided to enter as well. I pushed open the door and walked slowly inside. There were quite a number of people, about thirty or forty, and most of them were youths, men and girls from the ages of fourteen to nineteen, dressed impeccably in the new style which was the present rage. None of them was making any noise, they seemed to form part of a sort of a self-conscious ballet, and only the older people were laughing in that loud, forced way which always seems to associate itself with the offshoots of religious worship. The driver of the scarlet motor-cycle was taking off his gear in a corner of the hall and when he stood erect I saw

115

it was Roger Rout. For a moment I thought it better not to approach him, particularly since I was still in a pretty poor state.

At the back of the hall there was a small raised stage, and directly beside it the members of a small orchestra were seated, softly tuning up their electric guitars, teasing the drum and trickling over a piano. The vicar climbed up on to the stage and held up his hand. Immediately the fruit-machines stopped rattling their insides and there was complete quiet. At this point the vicar put his hand in his pocket, took out an enormous false red nose and attached it over his own. His action was greeted by silence, except for one obsequious titter from a middle-aged lady in a bulging hat. 'A funny thing happened to me just now as I was coming to the Mission Hall,' he said. 'I thought I was alone but I discovered I wasn't alone. And yet when I looked around I couldn't see anybody there. Can anybody explain that?' He looked appealingly at his audience. Nobody made a sound, and the silence became embarrassing, I even wanted to try and answer his question, when I saw a lot of nudging going on among the seats. Then a young girl with a red face got up and spoke in a piping voice.

'Jesus Christ,' she said, and sat down. The vicar looked pleased and raised his hand once more. There was a sound of applause. Rout took off his false nose, placed it back in his pocket and put on a serious face.

'Religion,' he said, 'is Fun. There is no need to have gloomy faces and snoop about as if you were at a funeral. Old people, of course, need religion—and I apologise to those of you here present over the age of twenty-two—but they don't need it so much as the Young, because the Older People are much nearer the greatest Fun Place of all, which is Heaven. Unless, of course, they go to the Other Place, where the jokes are really very bad. Therefore, Young People, enjoy yourselves. And what is the best way to enjoy yourselves?' He paused again and held up his hand.

There was another long silence before the same young girl got up from her chair and said, 'Service'.

'Precisely,' said the vicar. 'Service is the only way to enjoy yourself. And now, all joking aside, I want you all to enter the Army of God. I want you to wave good-bye to sin, to keep your thoughts as clean as your motor-cycles and leave each other strictly alone until you are married. You all know the penalties for not doing that. If you see dirty books or pictures, tell the police who are trying to look after you, and above all respect your parents and remember what they have done for you, and how much they have sacrificed. Now we'll have a slight interlude for refreshment.'

The vicar got down from the stage and the orchestra started playing. It was a good orchestra, with a good beat. It was interesting how the new England had caught the fever of music in its blood. The crowd of people in the hall stood about chatting and then one or two couples started dancing. All these couples were fairly old, and they seemed to be dancing the waltz to the music of a Blues number. When the music stopped the vicar returned to the stage. He was wearing his false nose and was carrying some coloured handkerchiefs and a silver ball.

'I want you to watch this very closely,' he began. After manoeuvring with two of the handkerchiefs the silver ball disappeared and then fell on the floor. This was followed by loud applause. 'All in the game,' said the vicar, and performed three more tricks. He then retired to the back of the hall while the orchestra struck up. At this point I decided to go over to him.

'I remember you,' said Rout. 'It was with Jonathan Glory. There was that unfortunate incident.'

'That's right,' I said.

'The unfortunate woman is now deceased, I hear,' he said.

'Yes,' I said, 'but I didn't want to talk to you about that.'

'I am, as you see, very busy,' said the vicar.

'You can't be too busy for what I've got to say,' I said. 'I'm in the most terrible trouble. There are people trying to kill me.'

'Kill you?' cried the vicar. 'In the name of Heaven, don't speak so loud.' He was seized with a fit of coughing. 'Who are trying to kill you?' He whispered.

'The Reservation gang,' I said. 'Glory is in it and I think Inspector Gladcliff is, and possibly Swinger.'

'Absolutely out of the question,' said Rout. 'Out of the question. For one thing, Glory frequently sends donations to my Mission Hall, and on two occasions he has sung a few songs for my little congregation. I can't believe it.' I told him shortly, what had happened and he shook his head slowly. 'If this is true, it's terrible,' he said. 'I've always been trying my best.' I looked at him closely and thought he looked frightened. 'There's absolutely nothing I can do to help you,' he said, 'nothing at all.'

There was a sudden shout from the other end of the hall.

'Police,' cried a voice. 'It's the Police.' The vicar moved forward uncomprehendingly. I followed him to the door. Two policemen stood outside.

'Excuse me, sir,' said the larger of the two, 'but are you the Reverend Roger Rout?'

'Indeed I am,' said the vicar.

'Then could you tell me if a certain Mr Anthony Carson is in the hall?'

118

'I am Anthony Carson,' I said.

'Then will you please accompany me to the police station. They wish to make some inquiries.' I followed the two policemen to their car.

On the way to the police station, the shorter policeman gave me some of the facts. 'It's murder,' he said. 'An individual named Jackson has killed an individual named Gold.'

Four

'JACKSON is here in one of the cells,' said the C.I.D. sergeant. 'This is an informal talk, you understand.'

'Certainly,' I said, 'I quite understand that.' That was certainly what I hoped.

'My name is Sedge,' said the sergeant in a very friendly voice.

'How do you do, Mr Sedge,' I said, and gave a rather complicated smile.

'The point is,' said Sedge, 'that it is generally known you were—are, possibly—one of Jackson's closest friends, and you may be called as a witness. But there is nothing to worry about.'

'He's a friend of mine,' I said. There was nothing else to say.

'You didn't actually witness Jackson killing Gold?' he asked.

'Certainly not,' I said. 'I was far away.' I decided to tell him about my movements and all my dubious relationships, except for the dark truth of Jackson's transformation.

'Another point,' said the sergeant. 'There are certain rumours. As far as I'm concerned, they are absolutely ridiculous. About certain people changing identity and that sort of lark. Have you heard anything about that?'

'Nothing at all,' I said. I had no hesitation in saying that.

'As far as we're concerned,' said Sedge, 'it's not to be even considered. We always get people on the lunatic fringe giving that sort of information. But please tell me something about you movements.' I decided to tell him most of the truth. He noted it down in a book.

'Glory and Inspector Gladcliff have been arrested,' said Sedge. 'We haven't touched the clergy.'

'Of course not,' I said.

'Marietti has been taken to hospital, but nobody gives him a chance.' He offered me a cigarette. 'There's something I'd like to tell you. The honest policeman is a hard-working man and he earns his money. And we're trying to be more honest every day.'

'I wouldn't like to be a policeman,' I said.

'You writers,' said Sedge.

I walked along the corridor and smiled at the Station sergeant. He didn't smile back. They never do. I remembered that from once being on a drunk and disorderly charge. Penelope Lingley was standing near the door and I walked over to her.

'I've just seen Jackson,' she said.

'It's ridiculous calling him Jackson, if you love him,' I said.

'You know why,' she said. 'He's getting out of it now. He's

doing the experiment. He's probably done it already. I brought him some straw, and I only hope it's the right kind.'

'If it works, you're alone,' I said, and looked down at the floor.

'That's true,' she said. I wanted to say we were both alone, but I didn't.

'He may be away already,' said Penelope.

'For his sake,' I said. 'I certainly hope he is.'

A policeman clumped along the corridor towards the sergeant. 'Sarge,' he cried, 'there's something odd going on down there in the cells.'

'What sort of odd?' said the sergeant, who seemed to be living in a hermetic sort of island of disapproval.

'It's a smell. A very strong sort of smell,' he said.

'Be more precise,' said the Sergeant. 'If you can.'

'It's a terrible smell of seaweed,' said the policeman.

'Seaweed,' snorted the sergeant.

Five

'THE question we have to ask ourselves,' said the judge, 'is whether, in fact, the accused did fire at Richard Gold in self-defence. It may seem unlikely that a quiet, well-behaved citizen like the deceased would deliberately provoke anyone to such an extent. Let alone an individual such as the defendant, whose character you are by now only too familiar with. I hardly need to stress the nature of this man and his background or go over the many appalling and sordid details which you have had to hear. Never before, in the course of my duty, have I presided over a case such as this one, possessing, as it does, so many sordid and infamous overtones.

'You will consider the known facts of the case, setting aside, if you can, prejudice and bias affected, only too easily, by the loathsome accumulation of these recorded crimes against society.' The judge looked for some time at the jury, his eyes moving from face to face as though he was trying to transmit his thoughts into each of their brains. Then he turned and looked at Jackson. It was a long, steady look, and it should hardly have been difficult for the jury to read a histrionic kind of disgust in his expression, however concealed by legal majesty.

The judge rose and the court rose. Before leaving the courtroom, the judge turned and looked at me and then at Penelope, who was standing beside me. On the other side of Penelope stood Stella, who was holding a handkerchief up to her eyes. She wasn't aware that the judge had turned his head to gaze at her.

'It's the end of Jackson,' Penelope whispered to me.

'There's nothing to be done now,' I said. Beyond telling the truth and turning night into day, catching the moon in a net and being born at the end of time. No true thing could be said, there was only the ritual of naming. An usher approached me.

'Mr Carson,' he said.

'Yes,' I said.

'This is for you,' he said, handing me an envelope. I opened it and took out a sheet of paper.

122

'Come round immediately to my chambers behind the court,' I read, 'and bring Penelope with you.'

'Who is this note from?' I asked the usher.

'From His Worship the Judge,' said the usher.

'I have to see him,' I said. 'Could you show me the way?'

We went along a corridor and climbed some stairs. The usher knocked at a door and then opened it. At first I did not recognise the judge, he had taken off his wig and was sipping a glass of sherry. 'Come inside and sit down,' he said, pointing to some chairs. Penelope and I sat down. 'There's no need to beat about the bush,' said the judge. 'I am Jackson.' He looked at both of us in turn. 'Or, if you prefer, Gold.' The three of us stared at one another in silence for a long time. Then, suddenly, as though a conductor's bâton had been raised, the three of us burst into laughter. It felt as though we couldn't stop, we were carried along by an enormous wave of laughter, choking in the foam. Then we stopped and remained quiet. I could hear a pigeon murmuring outside the window. 'Have some sherry,' said the judge.

'The main thing, now,' said the judge, 'is action. Don't you agree, Penelope?'

'I'm ready,' she said.

'We will conduct the experiment this very moment before the jury has considered its verdict. For obvious reasons. I do not want to sentence the accused.' There was another burst of laughter, but it was over in less than a minute. 'I need some straw,' said the judge. 'Any sort of straw will do.' He took hold of my arm. 'Get some as quickly as you can. Run all the way. Don't stop running.'

I rushed out of the room, down the stairs and through the main entrance to the court. I had no idea where to find any straw when I noticed a fruit shop on the other side of the street. I started to run, and half-way across I bumped into somebody. It was a woman. She seized me by the wrist, and I recognised Stella.

'Where are you going?' she cried. 'What's happening?'

'The judge asked to see me,' I said, without thinking.

'The judge,' she cried. 'But it's impossible. Judges don't see people in the middle of a trial. He doesn't even know you.'

'Stella,' I said, 'I'm in a terrible hurry. It's frightfully important. Please leave go of me at once.'

'You've got to tell me what's going on,' she shouted. 'Is it something about my husband?'

'It's a private matter,' I said.

'It must be about my husband,' said Stella. 'He may be a terrible man, but don't you see. I love him. I'll always love him.'

'Good-bye Stella,' I shouted, and ran towards the fruit shop.

'Straw,' I cried to the old woman who was filling a bag with peaches. 'Straw, any sort of straw.'

'Straw?' she said. 'What straw?'

'Any sort of old straw,' I said. 'I'll give you a pound for it. Here's the pound.'

'God save us,' she said, but she hurried to the back of the shop and came back with a huge armful. I threw the pound note on top of a box of apples, grabbed the straw and made my way back to the judge's chambers.

The judge took the straw off me directly I entered the room. He bundled it together and twisted it until I could see the faint resemblance of a bird. 'Have you got any string?' he asked.

'I haven't got any string,' I said.

'There isn't time to get any now,' said the judge. 'I'll have to manage without.' He worked on the straw for another couple of minutes and then stood up.

'Are you ready, Penelope?'

'Yes, darling,' said Penelope, 'I'll go anywhere with you.'

'Very well. Here goes.' He began speaking a fast flow of words in an incomprehensible language and then burnt a number of pieces of paper which he flung up, flaming into the air. I thought I heard a sound, something between a deep, drowned bell and a peal of thunder, and the room was suddenly filled with the smell of ozone. I could feel the wind and I could hear the wind, I was clinging to the table. At that moment the door opened and Stella walked in.

She rushed across the room. I could see the wind blowing her hair. I was very frightened. She stood in front of the judge and then fell on her knees.

'For God's sake, save my husband,' she cried. 'Save him. Save him.' There was the stun of an explosion, and then everything went black.

When I opened my eyes the room was empty except for Penelope. She was standing beside the open window, looking out. 'There they are,' she said in a calm voice, pointing. I looked up at the sky, and quite high up I could see two large white birds, their wide wings beating the rhythm of the wild, free winds.

ANTHONY CARSON,
London, 1964.